P9-CLC-019

FROM THE
NANCY DREW FILES

THE CASE: *The promise of adventure and romance may be broken—by the threat of death!*

CONTACT: *Franz Haussman is the heir to a Swiss watchmaking fortune—but he could be living on borrowed time.*

SUSPECTS: *Yves Petiau—The owner of a rival watchmaking firm, he wouldn't mind seeing Franz take a fall . . . off the Matterhorn.*

Erich Haussman—Franz's cousin, he has had to stand by while Franz stands to inherit the company and win over the beautiful Monique Montreux.

Mick Devlin—He's young, he's handsome, he's charming, and he claims his interest in Nancy is purely romantic . . . but his story has more holes than Swiss cheese.

COMPLICATIONS: *Nancy can't ignore her feelings of attraction toward Mick, but what if he's just using her to get to Franz? And what about Ned, back in the States?*

Books in The Nancy Drew Files® Series

Available from ARCHWAY Paperbacks

The Nancy Drew Files™

PASSPORT TO ROMANCE

Case 72

Swiss Secrets

Carolyn Keene

AN ARCHWAY PAPERBACK
Published by POCKET BOOKS
New York London Toronto Sydney Tokyo Singapore

AN ARCHWAY PAPERBACK *Original*

An Archway Paperback published by
POCKET BOOKS, a division of Simon & Schuster Inc.
1230 Avenue of the Americas, New York, NY 10020

Copyright © 1992 by Simon & Schuster Inc.
Produced by Mega-Books of New York, Inc.

ISBN: 0-671-73076-2

First Archway Paperback printing June 1992

10 9 8 7 6 5 4 3 2 1

NANCY DREW, AN ARCHWAY PAPERBACK and colophon
are registered trademarks of Simon & Schuster Inc.

THE NANCY DREW FILES is a trademark
of Simon & Schuster Inc.

Cover art by Tricia Zimic

Printed in the U.S.A.

IL 6+

Swiss Secrets

Chapter

One

"Pinch me, Nancy!"

Nancy Drew glanced up from the guidebook in her hand. "What did you say, Bess?" she asked.

"Pinch me," repeated her friend, Bess Marvin. "I want to make sure this is really happening and we're really here."

"I know what you mean," said Bess's cousin George Fayne. A tall girl with short brown curls and the build of a natural athlete, George took in the hordes of travelers streaming past them in the Geneva-Cointrin Airport. "It's great to be in Switzerland at last."

"Absolutely!" Bess agreed. "Listen!" She pointed at a loudspeaker from which someone was announcing flight arrivals. "That's real Swiss!"

1

Nancy grinned. "Actually, that's real French, Bess. They speak French, German, and Italian here, not Swiss. Well, there is another language, which is very old, called Romansh, but it's not spoken by many people." She cast a quick glance around them. "What do you say, guys? Shall we get our bags and find out where to catch a train into Geneva."

Geneva was the girls' first stop in a summer of traveling in Europe. They had decided to start their trip in the Alps and had been lucky to get a good deal on tickets to Geneva. They weren't sure where they'd go from there. Rome, maybe? Spain or Greece? There were a few places they definitely wanted to see, but they had agreed to leave room to follow whatever adventures might come their way.

One thing was for sure—the girls' hometown of River Heights, in the Midwest, seemed a world away right then.

"Did you really need *four* suitcases, Bess?" George asked her cousin while they waited for their luggage to appear on the baggage carousel.

Bess smiled sheepishly. "I guess it *is* a lot, but I've got to compete with all those chic European girls, don't I?" she protested, fluffing out her long blond hair. "I just hope I look sophisticated enough for European guys."

"You always look great, Bess," Nancy reassured her. "Guys will be falling all over you, as usual—once we change out of these rumpled clothes, I mean." She glanced down at her own khaki pants and beige linen jacket, both a bit the worse for wear at the moment.

Bess shot Nancy a sidelong glance. "Speaking of guys, I'll bet you wish Ned were here."

Nancy's lips tightened in a straight line. She and Ned Nickerson, her longtime boyfriend, hadn't parted on the best of terms. "I don't want Ned to be here if *he* doesn't want to be here," she said in a voice tinged with irritation. "He's gotten so serious about his summer job at the insurance company that he felt he couldn't take any time off to come."

Nancy fell silent, staring blankly at the suit-cases cascading out onto the carousel.

"I bet Ned's already regretting that he didn't come," George said to comfort her. "What I'm concerned about is Kevin." A worried look came into her brown eyes as she added, "He travels so much that I hardly got to see him this month before leaving. I'm afraid that being away from him for a whole summer will *really* kill our relationship."

Nancy gave George's arm a sympathetic squeeze. George had been going out with Kevin Davis, a sports announcer, for the past few months.

"Cheer up, you two!" Beth said brightly. "We're going to be surrounded by cute European guys all summer. And you know what they say about continental men— Hey, there's one of my bags!"

Twenty minutes later the girls were struggling

to maneuver a horribly overloaded luggage carrier through the airport crowds. They were searching for an information booth, so they could get directions into Geneva. Bess was pulling the carrier, and Nancy and George were doing their best to keep the barely balanced luggage from toppling to the floor.

"Pardon, madame. Pardon, monsieur," Nancy apologized as the three girls kept careening into groups of travelers.

Bess half turned to Nancy. "Nancy, are you sure we're going in the right direction?" she asked. "I think we're— Oof!"

Bess plowed straight into a handsome young man, who lurched sideways. With a startled cry, he grabbed at the luggage carrier to steady himself. The carrier veered sideways, too, and toppled over, spilling the suitcases on top of him.

"Oh, no!" Bess's voice was filled with dismay. "How terrible! Here, let me help you up." Scarlet faced, she reached out to the young man, while Nancy and George hurried to collect the suitcases before passersby tripped over them.

"It was nothing, I assure you." Grasping Bess's hand, the young man sprang lightly to his feet. He kept her hand in his a second longer than necessary, then smiled charmingly at all three girls. "Since the suitcases seem to have broken the ice for us, let me introduce myself. I am Franz Haussman."

Nancy couldn't help thinking of Bess's remark about continental men. Franz Haussman could

4

only be a few years older than she was. Yet—
from his silk jacket to his sleek leather loafers—
he was dressed with the kind of elegance she
rarely saw in the guys she knew at home. He had
a slim but muscular build and reddish brown
hair that was long on top and trimmed stylishly
short at the sides and in back. His hazel eyes
danced with merriment.

"Sorry I was so clumsy," Franz went on in a
voice that had only a slight tinge of an accent. "I
was not paying attention. May I help you gather
your things?"

"I think we've got it under control," Bess
commented as George gingerly balanced the last
suitcase on top of the pile. From the sparkle in
Bess's pale blue eyes, Nancy could tell that she
had noticed how gorgeous Franz was.

"May I escort you to wherever you are going?
Really, you must let me help," Franz insisted.

"Well, we *are* trying to figure out how to get
into Geneva," Bess told him. "Do you have any
idea where we catch the train?"

Franz Haussman's smile broadened. "But of
course I do," he said with a twinkle in his eye. "I
am en route to the same train. It is only a
six-minute ride into Geneva, you will find. However, I must inform you that you are going the
wrong way. Please allow me to lead you down to
the train.

"Is this your first visit to Switzerland?" he
inquired as he deftly turned the luggage carrier
around for them. When the girls nodded, he said,

5

"Well, you will enjoy yourselves tremendously here. I am always happy to return home."

"So, you live in Geneva?" Bess asked.

Franz nodded. "Yes, but I am just now returning from Monaco. You must try to go there if you can—especially if you like gambling."

"Gambling?" Bess echoed.

"But of course," Franz said. "Monaco is famous for its gambling, you know. The casinos were very, very good to me this time."

Nancy didn't want to get involved with any gambling and was relieved when Franz changed the subject, asking what the girls were doing in Geneva. Nancy grinned as Bess launched into the story of their trip. There was no doubt about it—Bess had a crush on Franz already.

"Nancy's been so busy with her cases that I wasn't sure we'd *ever* get here," Bess said before Nancy could stop her. "You know, she's a very famous detective back home."

For a split second Franz Haussman gave Nancy an edgy glance. Then he recovered his easy charm and smiled broadly. Nancy wondered if she'd imagined his discomfort.

"A detective?" Franz repeated casually. "How —unusual. I hope you are not working on your trip," he said gallantly. "It would be a pity to spoil your first visit to Geneva."

Then quickly changing the subject, Franz said, "I am meeting a friend tonight at a club on Lake Geneva. Would you care to join us?"

"Let's!" Bess exclaimed, her blue eyes sparkling as she turned to George and Nancy.

George nodded readily. "I'm game," she said.

"Sounds great. We're up for anything," Nancy agreed, smiling at Franz Haussman. "Just do me one favor, though—tell us *exactly* how to find the club from our hotel. If we got lost in the airport, who knows what might happen once we actually get to the city!"

"This place is just as gorgeous as I thought it would be." Bess sighed, staring out the taxi window.

The three girls said goodbye to Franz after their train had arrived in Geneva's Gare Cornevin. Now they were on their way to the hotel they had chosen from one of their guidebooks.

As Nancy gazed out at the streets of Geneva, she felt pretty excited herself. The city was beautiful—a combination of a medieval storybook town and a sleekly futuristic city. Gabled, turreted houses stood next to glass-fronted office buildings, and narrow cobblestoned streets alternated with smooth paved ones. The people they passed looked happy, everything was spotless, and Lake Geneva was a dazzling expanse of blue.

"Wow!" Bess said as they passed a massive fountain of water shooting up out of the lake.

"That's the Jet d'Eau—a jet of water," their taxi driver told her, half turning in his seat to talk to the girls. "It is more than four hundred feet high and is our most famous landmark."

Soon after, the taxi pulled up in front of the Hôtel du Lac, which was on a quiet street a couple of blocks from Lake Geneva. Nancy was glad to see that although the building was modest, the hotel was pleasant and welcoming, with neatly tended window boxes and a small but clean lobby.

"You check us in, okay, Nan?" George murmured under her breath as the three girls approached the desk. "My French is a little weak."

Nancy, too, felt a bit uneasy. She'd taken lots of French in school, but suddenly it all seemed to disappear.

"*Bonjour, mesdemoiselles,*" said a smiling, apple-cheeked young woman at the desk. "*Puis-je vous aider?*"

That part Nancy understood at least. The clerk was asking if she could help them. "*Oui, merci,*" Nancy replied. "*Nous—uh—nous—*"

"*Nous vouloir* to check in," Bess added helpfully.

"Bess, you just said, 'We to want to check in'!" Nancy whispered.

Luckily the clerk smiled her understanding. She slid a register across the counter to the girls, who signed it gratefully. Then she riffled through some papers, found a key, and handed it to Nancy. "*Quarante-deux,*" she said.

Since the number on the key was 42, Nancy

figured the clerk had been telling them their room number. *"Merci beaucoup,"* Nancy said. Then she turned to her friends. "What do you say we unpack and then maybe take a look around?" she suggested.

"And get something to eat," George added. "I'm starving."

"Starving? I know just the place," came a man's voice from behind them.

Startled, the three girls turned around. For the second time that day Nancy found herself facing a handsome young man. He was tall—at least six foot three, Nancy guessed—and blond, with a rangy build, broad shoulders, and the greenest eyes Nancy had ever seen. He was dressed in well-worn jeans, a black T-shirt, and leather sneakers. Except for his accent, Nancy would have taken him for a fellow American.

"I'm Mick Devlin," the guy said. "I'm an Aussie—from Australia, that is. You're Americans, eh? And this is your first trip to Switzerland."

Nancy found that she couldn't stop staring into his deep green eyes. She was grateful when George spoke up. "Well, you're right," George said, laughing. "I can't believe it's so obvious that this is all new to us."

"But that's great!" Mick said, grinning. "Let me show you around. You don't know it yet, but you picked a great part of town to stay in. Let's see," he added. "We'll start by getting you some

9

food. Bread and cheese at a fantastic bakery right across the street. Then we'll head up to the rue du Marché and take a walk around the Vieille Ville— that's the Old City. If there's time, we'll see the European headquarters of the United Nations and go shopping on the Left Bank and take a look at the flower clock and visit my favorite spot in Geneva—the Watch and Clock Museum. Geneva's the watchmaking center of Switzerland, you know—"

"Whoa!" Bess exclaimed, holding up a hand. "You sure know the city. Do you live here?"

"Oh, no," Mick said lightly. "Just passing through. I'm a tourist, like yourselves. But I've been here for a few days."

Nancy was impressed by how well he seemed to have learned Geneva. "It all sounds great, but we just got off the plane," she told Mick. "We need a little time to unwind before we start hitting the tourist attractions."

"Okay," Mick agreed with an easy grin. "I'll give you ten minutes. If you're interested, come back down then and meet me here in the lobby. If you don't show, I'll figure you're napping instead."

It was a tactful way to avoid seeming too pushy, Nancy thought. After exchanging a quick glance with Bess and George, she told him, "We'll definitely meet you here in ten minutes. And thanks very much, Mick."

* * *

"I don't suppose this stuff is for sale, is it?" asked a wistful Bess later that day. She was gazing down at an exquisitely jeweled gold clock shaped like a tiny stagecoach. The three girls and Mick were standing in the Musée de l'Horlogerie—the Watch and Clock Museum. The charming châ teau was filled with four centuries' worth of timepieces.

Mick laughed. "I don't think we could afford it if it were. Still, it is a nice museum, eh?"

All three girls nodded enthusiastically. "It's great of you to show us all around like this," Nancy told Mick appreciatively. "We've had a perfect first day here, thanks to you."

Mick smiled at her, and for some reason Nancy felt a tingle of excitement run down her spine. "It's been perfect for me, too," he said. "Now all we have to do is decide where to go after this to make it even more perfect."

After a picnic lunch in a beautiful park near their hotel, Mick had taken the girls to the Reformation Monument, a massive three-hundred-foot stone wall adorned with stern-looking statues of Protestant Reformation leaders. From there they had gone to the European headquarters of the United Nations and to the Museum of Art and History, before heading to the Watch and Clock Museum.

"How'd you find out about all these places?" George asked Mick as they moved into another jewellike room in the Watch and Clock Museum.

"You've obviously memorized your guide-books."

"Geneva's a place I've wanted to visit for a long time," Mick said, shrugging. "I guess I *did* do a lot of studying."

"Your French is certainly good," Nancy commented. "Have you been to Europe before?"

Mick didn't answer. Instead, he checked his watch and looked up at her with an eager smile. "Hey, how about a walk along the waterfront now? We could get a spot of dinner afterward . . ."

Nancy checked her own watch. "Oh, Mick, I'm sorry," she said, with genuine regret, "but we have to go out tonight. We should probably go back to the hotel and change."

"Leaving me so soon?" Mick asked. "Well, let's go find the bus back to the hotel, then." There was a note of clownish regret in his voice, but his expression was genuinely disappointed. His eyes strayed back to Nancy for an instant, and again she felt unaccountably excited.

Mick found a bus that dropped them off a block from their hotel. As they began to cross the street, Nancy caught sight of a tiny newsstand on the corner. "Hang on a sec," she said. "I want to buy a paper to test my French."

Darting across to the newsstand, she fished in her purse for some Swiss francs and bought the evening paper. As she headed back toward her friends, she glanced down at the front page.

Nancy caught her breath. She recognized the

page one photograph—it was of Franz Haussman!

"Hey, guys!" Nancy called, racing over to her friends. "Look at this!"

Even with his expression of murderous rage, Franz Haussman was instantly recognizable. He was dressed in a tuxedo, and was punching a tall, bearded man smack in the face in front of a group of horrified onlookers.

"Isn't that Franz Haussman?" Bess asked.

George was staring at the article, too. "I assume Franz isn't punching that guy out because they're such good friends—right?"

"Franz Haussman would *never* punch anyone out," Bess said staunchly, glaring at her cousin. "I bet they doctored that photo."

"Who *is* Franz Haussman?" Mick wanted to know.

"I'll tell you in a sec," Nancy told him. "Let me just try to translate this."

She cleared her throat and began. "'Franz Haussman, the young'—uh—'heir of Frères Haussman'—that's Haussman Brothers. It must be the family business or something—"

"I've heard of Frères Haussman," Mick put in. "They make watches—really expensive ones."

"Wow. Well, this goes on to say that Franz—um—'evidently had trouble controlling himself at'—at—I can't figure out where it was, some ball or something—'the other evening,'" Nancy read. "'On the other hand, perhaps he doesn't need the art of—of' mastering himself? Oh!

13

'Self-control!—perhaps he doesn't need the art of self-control the way ordinary people do. After all, he is the—'"

Nancy gulped as she stared down at the page. "Am I reading this right?" she asked in amazement.

"The heir to the biggest fortune in Switzerland!"

Chapter

Two

NANCY STARED AT her friends in shocked silence.

"Whoa!" George said. "Trust Bess to get a crush on the richest guy in the country!"

Mick looked exasperatedly at the three girls. "Could one of you *please* explain what's going on?"

"Oh—sorry, Mick," Nancy said quickly, then briefly told him about the way they'd met Franz.

"What else does it say?" Bess asked eagerly.

Concentrating on the French text, Nancy said, "Okay. The guy Franz is punching is Yves Petiau. He's a—wait a sec—a 'son of his works.' What's that? Must mean some kind of self-made man or something. A millionaire, it says."

"So what's his problem with Franz?" George wanted to know.

"Something about watches," Nancy told her. "Franz accused Petiau of using the Haussman name on his cheap imitation watches. It says here that Franz started the fight and that it's not the first time he's attracted notoriety. Then it goes on to say how some society lady called Franz a disgrace to his family and an impetuous child."

"No way," Bess said indignantly. "I *know* he's a good guy. He'll prove it when we see him tonight."

"He's the guy you're meeting tonight?" Mick asked, surprised. "You girls really move fast!"

Nancy grinned up at him, and a sudden thought occurred to her. "Why don't you come with us, Mick?" she said. "I'm sure Franz won't mind if you come, too."

"You think so?" Mick asked quizzically. "He wouldn't punch *me* in the nose?"

"Of course not," Bess told him. "He's a great guy. That's what we're trying to tell you!"

Mick smiled at Bess's remark, but his eyes were fixed on Nancy's face. "If you want me along, then sure, I'd love to come," he said. "When and where should I meet you? In the lobby? Eight? Nine?"

They settled on eight. Mick had an errand to run and strode off down the street while the girls made their way back to the hotel.

"Well, that makes *two* great-looking guys we've met so far," Bess said, trying to keep up with

Nancy and George. "And they're both so nice! It'll be fun having Mick come with us tonight."

"I'm sure *Nancy* thinks so," George said, fixing Nancy with a sly look. "At least, I'm sure Mick will be happy to spend more time with you, Nan. Did you notice how he kept staring at you?"

Nancy felt herself blushing. "He did not!"

"Yes, he did," Bess and George said in unison. "But we won't torture you about it," Bess added diplomatically. "The *really* important thing is, what are we going to wear to the club tonight? I don't think I brought anything that's right."

The girls had decided that the easiest way to save money on their trip was on their accommodations. As a result, their hotel room was barely big enough for the three of them to change in at the same time. When Mick's eyes widened as he met them in the lobby, Nancy knew they'd achieved the effect they'd been hoping for even in a cramped space. She was wearing a black, backless minidress, Bess was in a pink silk dress with spaghetti straps, and George wore a red sheath with a wide black belt.

"You all look great," Mick said appreciatively. "I'm treating you to a cab—no arguments, please. Those outfits just weren't meant for public transportation."

By night Geneva was even more exciting and festive than it had been during the day. When they passed the waterfront, Nancy noticed dozens of people strolling by Lake Geneva. The sparkling lights of cruise boats moved slowly back and forth over the water.

"Those boats are called *mouettes genevoises.* They're like water buses," Mick explained.

"You should be a tour guide," Nancy said in amazement. "How do you know so much about —Wait, I bet this is the club."

Their cab was pulling up in front of a building that looked more like a massive black, window-less box than anything else. A sign above the door read Le Monde in bold lettering. Photographers were standing guard outside the entrance, cameras at the ready to catch anyone who might be famous. All kinds of people were streaming in and out of the club—kids in tattered T-shirts and jeans, sleek and elegant jet-setters, and even what looked like the members of a soccer team having a little postgame fun.

"This is great!" Bess was already halfway out of the cab. "Come on, you guys—hurry!"

"Wow!" said all three girls simultaneously the instant they were inside the club.

Before them was a room that was about the size of a roller-skating rink. Colored lights lit up its translucent dance floor, and the walls had been covered with a heat-sensitive fabric that changed color when touched. A floodlit indoor waterfall was coursing down one entire wall of the room. Nancy was amazed to see that real trees—hung with huge, flamboyant plastic birds —were growing right out of the floor.

"Welcome to Le Monde—the best club in

Geneva!" Nancy turned to see Franz Haussman at her elbow. He was speaking loudly to be heard over the rock music that was blasting in the background. "We've been waiting for you!"

He turned to a pretty, dark-haired girl standing at his side. She had a tangled mass of ringlets and huge, dark eyes. "This is my girlfriend, Monique Montreux," Franz said.

Nancy hoped that she was the only one who had witnessed Bess's disappointment. Still, Monique struck Nancy as being very nice. "Welcome to Switzerland," Monique was saying warmly. She hesitated slightly over the English words. "How was your first day in Geneva?"

"Wonderful," Nancy replied. "Of course we had a tour guide with us," she added with a smile. "Franz, this is Mick Devlin. Mick, meet Franz Haussman and Monique Montreux."

Mick and Franz exchanged a polite greeting, but Monique's eyes widened at the sight of Mick. "We have met before, no?" she asked in a puzzled, heavily accented voice.

Nancy was almost sure she saw Mick blush, though the light was too dim to be certain. "Don't think so," Mick said gruffly.

"But I'm sure I have seen you," Monique insisted. "Could it have been at—"

This time Mick cut her off before she could finish. "You must have me mixed up with someone else," he said brusquely. "We've never met."

Nancy shot him a quick glance, her detective's instincts aroused. She couldn't help thinking that

19

Mick sounded as though he were hiding something. Quit it! she ordered herself in the next instant. You're on vacation, Drew!

"How is your hotel?" Franz asked, cutting through Nancy's thoughts.

George exchanged a grin with Nancy and Bess. "Oh, it's very comfortable. It has a stunning view of a brick wall, but we have no complaints."

"Well, let me show you the view in here," said Franz, chuckling. "Perhaps you will find it more interesting."

Now Nancy realized that the dance area they were in was surrounded by hallways leading to other rooms. Led by Franz and Monique, the girls and Mick threaded their way through the dancers and headed down one hallway.

"Meet the sixties," Franz said, ushering them into the room at the end of the hall.

Nancy blinked in amazement. They were in a room that looked as if it had come straight out of 1967. The walls were covered with a huge paisley print in Day-Glo colors and beanbag chairs were scattered on the floor. Couples wearing patched blue jeans, leather vests, peace signs, and beaded necklaces were dancing to an old song.

"This is great!" Nancy said enthusiastically. "Does every room in this club have a theme?"

"Of course," Franz said, looking pleased by her reaction. "Let's see—I could take you to the punk room now. Or perhaps the rap room? Or the heavy metal dungeon? There is something for everyone."

Nancy was amazed as Franz led her and her friends through the rooms. Each one could have been an entire club in itself. "And now for the diner," Franz said proudly. He led the group to a perfect replica of a 1950s diner—complete with gum-snapping waitresses and milk shakes.

"Isn't this perfect?" he asked as a waitress seated them at a booth covered in turquoise vinyl. "They have authentic American food! I thought you would be glad to have a taste of home."

Nancy exchanged an amused look with her friends. "Franz, we're in Europe to learn *new* things. We should be having—I don't know— squid or eels or something."

The girls had snatched a quick supper at the hotel before leaving, so they only ordered milk shakes—which did taste great. In a few minutes everyone was talking animatedly.

"You know, Franz," George said, scooping up some of her chocolate shake, "I still don't know what you do."

"Oh, all kinds of things," Franz told her brightly. "I have a great job working for the family business. They're letting me—"

He broke off as the pulsing beat of the song in the main dance hall grew extremely loud and drowned out his words. "They must have cranked up the volume to get people to dance. I'll tell you later," Franz shouted.

"*We're* close enough to talk," Mick said, leaning in to Nancy. "You can hear me, right?"

"Right, but I'll only listen if you tell me something interesting," she said, teasing him.

Mick gave her a devilish smile. "No fear, love. You won't be able to tear yourself away."

"Oh, is that so?" Nancy's blue eyes were sparkling. "You haven't said much this evening. In fact, you've been awfully easy to ignore."

"In that case, you'd better have a dance with me. Then you'll *have* to pay attention to me."

Nancy hadn't flirted with anyone in a long time. She was surprised at how easy—and fun— it could be. "All right, Devlin," she said, jumping to her feet. "I'll take you up on that. Which room do you want to dance in?"

"How about the main dance floor?" Mick suggested. "The smaller rooms are fun, but there's nothing like good old rock 'n' roll."

Nancy turned to everyone else. "Anyone else care to join us on the dance floor?" she shouted.

"Give us a chance to finish our food first!" Franz shouted back, gesturing to his burger.

Monique rolled her eyes. "I suppose I must wait for Franz," she said jokingly.

Bess and George decided to sit out the song. For a second Nancy wondered about waiting to dance herself, but the music from the main dance area was pulsating through the whole club, and she couldn't resist it any longer.

"Just as I suspected," Mick said a few minutes later. "You're a great dancer."

"You are, too." Suddenly Nancy felt almost shy. It was a little strange to be having such a good time with someone who—well, who wasn't Ned.

"Do you want to dance the next one?" Mick asked. "Or we could—"

Suddenly someone tugged desperately at Nancy's arm. She turned to see Bess standing next to her, an expression of horror on her face.

"Nancy! Come quickly!" Bess cried. "Something terrible has happened!"

"What? What is it?" Without giving a thought to Mick, Nancy raced off the dance floor.

"This way," Bess shouted, pulling Nancy toward the hall that led to the American diner. "There!" Bess pointed a shaky finger down the hall.

Franz Haussman was lying on the floor, motionless. His face was deathly pale, and blood streamed from his nose, drenching his shirt. A sobbing Monique was kneeling next to him.

"Oh, no! What happened?" Nancy gasped.

As she raced toward Franz, pushing through a gathering crowd, a blond, burly man shoved past her and disappeared into the main dance area.

"That's the guy!" Bess cried, pointing at the heavyset man. "He's the one who threatened to kill Franz!"

Chapter

Three

"THAT MAN DID a lot more than threaten," Nancy said grimly, bending over Franz. She was relieved to see that he was still conscious, though he was obviously in pain.

"That's a nasty bloody nose, Franz," Nancy said. "Are you hurt anywhere else?"

Franz gave her a wan smile. "Just my pride," he answered as he struggled to sit up. He looked behind Nancy and spoke briefly in French. *"C'est fini.* The show is over, everyone. I am fine."

The crowd of curious spectators began to drift away. Mick was standing right next to Nancy, and she found his presence oddly comforting.

"Franz, do you know who that man was who attacked you?" Nancy asked as Monique dabbed

24

with a tissue at his bloody face. "Did you do anything to make him angry?"

"Nothing," Franz replied, but Nancy noticed a flicker of unease in his eyes. "All I did was walk toward the dance floor with Monique. That man must be one of your father's henchmen, hired to hurt me," he said to his girlfriend.

Monique stared at Franz in horror. "No, it could not be," she whispered hoarsely. "Papa would never hire anyone to hurt you."

"Here," Mick said, stepping forward and bending over Franz. "Let's take you to the men's room and clean you up a bit." With a steadying arm around Franz's shoulders, Mick led him away.

When the two guys were gone, Monique turned to Nancy. "Papa would never want Franz hurt," she said again. "He is—he is very angry about our situation, but to hire someone to hurt Franz? Impossible!"

"Angry about what situation?" Bess asked.

"Let's all sit down somewhere," Nancy put in gently. "Monique is upset, and no wonder. Shall we go back to the diner?"

Monique shook her head. "Too noisy, but there is a quiet lounge where we can talk," she said. "But how will Franz know where we are?"

"I'll wait here for him and Mick," Bess offered.

"That would be great," Nancy said. "Where's George, by the way?"

"Oh, a cute guy asked her to dance," Bess told

her. "I think they're in the sixties room. I'm sure she'll find us when she needs to."

Monique led Nancy to a lounge that was decorated like a proper British drawing room. A few couples were talking in low voices at one end of the room, but they paid no attention as Nancy and Monique sank down on a sofa.

"Are you all right?" she asked Monique.

"N-not really. It was so hard to see Franz attacked like that and to hear him accuse *Father* of wanting him hurt." Monique's voice wavered, and she fumbled in her bag for a handkerchief.

"You see," she continued, gazing earnestly at Nancy, "Papa wants Franz and me to—to settle down. So do Franz's parents, of course. They only want what is best for us, but they can be very . . . harsh at times. We come from two old, wealthy families. My father owns Montreux Chocolates, and—well, naturally they would like us to marry."

"I've heard of Montreux Chocolates," Nancy said. "They're supposed to be fabulous."

Monique nodded distractedly. "We'll have to make sure that you try some," she said politely. "Anyway, Papa says he is tired of my spending time with a man like Franz unless we are going to marry. He never stops talking about it."

"Well, what are *your* feelings about Franz?" Nancy asked gently. "Do you think you're wasting your time?"

Monique snapped her head around to look at Nancy, her long brown curls bouncing from the

26

sudden motion. "No! That's just it!" she cried. "We want to get married but not yet. I'm not ready to settle down, either. But my parents don't believe that. They think I'm protecting Franz."

Nancy felt a rush of gratitude that her own father, Carson Drew, was so understanding. She hesitated a moment before asking Monique, "Then how can you be sure your parents *aren't* behind this attack on Franz?"

"Papa would never hire anyone to beat up Franz! What would be the point?"

"There *is* no point," came Franz's voice from behind the girls. "You are right, Monique. I've been thinking about it." He was standing in the doorway with Mick, Bess, and George. Franz looked much better now, despite the splotches of blood that remained on his shirt. While the rest of the group pulled up chairs, he sat down on the sofa next to Monique and took her hands in his.

"It was wrong of me to accuse your father like that," he said. "He may not like our relationship, but he is a fair person. Forgive me?"

"Of course I do." Monique beamed at him, and Nancy could tell that they had forgotten everyone else in the room for that moment.

"I hate to butt in," Nancy said cautiously, "but if the man who punched you *wasn't* hired by Monique's father, do you have any idea who he is?"

A momentary flicker of fear crossed Franz's eyes, but vanished so quickly Nancy was sure no one else had noticed it. He hesitated before answering. "Of course I don't know who he is," he said lightly. "Do I look like the kind of man who has enemies?"

No, you don't, Nancy wanted to tell him, but the newspaper implied you have plenty of them.

Before she could think of a tactful way to ask Franz about the newspaper article, a young man burst into the lounge and stormed over to the group. He had the same reddish brown hair as Franz, but he was thinner and more angular, with a stern look on his face.

"I've been looking all over for you!" the young man said to Franz, frowning. "Then I find out that someone *attacked* you! Monique, are you all right? What is going on?"

"Of course we'd like to know the answer to that question too, Erich," Franz said casually. "But more important than that, I'd like to introduce you to some new friends I've made." Sidestepping Erich's question, Franz introduced Nancy, Bess, George, and Mick. "And this is my cousin, Erich Haussman. He is always looking out for me," Franz added with a sarcastic edge to his voice.

"And *you* are always making new friends." The edge in Erich's voice was just as sharp, but Nancy noticed that he wasn't even looking at his cousin. Instead, he was staring at Monique, and the longing in his eyes contrasted sharply with his angry words. "You are so busy making friends that it is left to me to run *your* share of the business."

Bess seemed to be as uncomfortable as Nancy with witnessing this argument. "Um, do you two work together?" Bess asked, trying to diffuse the tension.

"We're supposed to," Erich told her in a biting voice. "Our parents thought it would be nice for us to help with the advertising for the family business, Frères Haussman. We make watches. Franz went to art school, so he is responsible for the so-called creative side of things. He works with the agencies to develop advertising campaigns, and then he forgets about them. I went to the *faculté de commerce*—business school in English—so I take care of all the boring details and finish the projects Franz drops."

Nancy felt uncomfortable and didn't know what to say, but Erich didn't seem to care what he said. "Speaking of cleaning up, Franz," he continued, "have you taken care of the Monaco question?"

Franz winced, and Nancy didn't know whether it was from pain or the sting of his cousin's words. "I've been busy," Franz said. "I will get to it tomorrow."

"Forget it," Erich muttered. "I will take care of it myself. You should get some rest after what happened to you tonight."

This sounded like a longstanding family quarrel, and Nancy wished she and her friends hadn't gotten caught in the middle of it. Mick must have felt the same way, for he suddenly glanced at his watch and said, "Time for me to go, or I'll turn into a pumpkin." He looked at Nancy, Bess, and George. "Would any of you like to catch a cab back to the hotel with me? Or shall I head out all alone into the dark, cold night?" he asked, his voice pulsing with mock tragedy.

"It's eleven!" Nancy said quickly. "I had no idea. I think I'll head back, too, Mick. The jet lag is starting to hit me."

Bess and George quickly chimed in their agreement. Nancy was sure that they, too, wanted to escape from this awkward situation. Still, it had been nice of Franz to invite them, and the four of them thanked him heartily.

"Take it easy with that nose of yours," George said jokingly as they turned to leave. "Don't walk into any walls."

"I'm sure he will," Erich put in. "He's good at getting into trouble—or hadn't you noticed?"

"Whew!" Bess said when she, Nancy, and George were finally back in their hotel room. "That got kind of heavy, didn't it? I hate family quarrels. Erich seems like a loser, especially compared to Franz." Letting out a long sigh, she added, "I guess Monique realizes how wonderful Franz is, too. Too bad. I guess I'll have to find a fabulous European romance somewhere else."

"I'm not sure Erich's a loser, exactly, but he certainly wasn't much fun to be around," George said, kicking off her heels. "I wonder how he and Franz can stand working together if they get on each other's nerves like that."

"Judging from their performance tonight, they *can't* stand it," said Nancy. She slipped off her dress and changed into her nightshirt, then went into the bathroom to wash up. "Did you notice that Erich seems to have a crush on Monique?" she called out to her friends.

"Always the detective," Bess teased. "*I* was too busy noticing what a crush Mick has on you to think about the Haussmans."

Nancy felt a little embarrassed. "He's a nice guy," was all she said. She splashed water on her face, relieved that her friends couldn't see the blush she felt rising to her cheeks.

"And cute," George put in slyly.

"And cute," Nancy agreed. "But don't get any ideas, you guys. Just because I had a few dances with him doesn't mean I'm in love." She dried her face, then went back into the bedroom. "We're almost forgetting about Franz getting attacked," she said, hastily changing the subject. "Bess, what exactly did the man who hit him say?"

Bess squinted as she tried to remember. "All I heard were a few words. The music was really loud at that point. But how much did he *have* to say? 'I'm going to kill you' gets right to the point, doesn't it?" She shivered. "The Montreux family must be horrible! Can you imagine hiring someone to beat up your daughter's boyfriend?"

"No, I can't," Nancy said, frowning. "Especially after hearing Monique talk about her father. Maybe that's not what happened."

George stared at Nancy blankly. "Well, what do you think *did* happen?"

"I wish I knew," said Nancy. "Franz acted a little weird when I asked if there was anyone else who might want to hurt him. I have a hunch there's something he's not telling us."

Suddenly Bess let out an enormous yawn. "Can—we—talk—about—this—tomorrow?" she asked groggily. "I'm so tired I'm ready to fall asleep standing up."

"Good idea, Bess," said Nancy. "I'm beat, too."

After they had all climbed into bed, Nancy tried to organize her thoughts. Was there any pattern to the events at the club? What was going on between Erich and Franz and Monique? And who on earth had attacked Franz so viciously?

Strangely, though, Nancy couldn't keep her thoughts focused on Franz. Try as she might, they kept drifting away. Her last thought before she fell asleep wasn't about Franz *or* the attack. Her last thought was of a funny, extraordinarily cute guy from Australia.

Chapter

Four

Voici vos petits déjeuners, mesdemoiselles."

"What did she say?" Bess asked in a whisper. It was Monday morning, and the girls were sitting in the hotel's cheerful, sunny dining room.

"She said our breakfast is here," Nancy replied as the waitress put their breakfast down on the table—fresh, flaky croissants, a pot of butter, a little dish of jam, and the richest-looking hot chocolate Nancy had ever seen.

"So, guys, remind me what's on the agenda for today," Bess said, heaping jam on her croissant. "That walking tour, right?"

Before Nancy or George could answer, the waitress reappeared at their table and handed Nancy an envelope. *"C'est pour vous, mademoiselle. L'enveloppe vient d'arriver."*

"Merci," Nancy said. "This just came," she said, translating for her friends. Curious, she opened the envelope and skimmed the brief message inside. "Hey, change of plans, guys!" she said. "Franz has invited us to go water-skiing on Lake Geneva at his parents' summer house."

"Fantastic!" George exclaimed. "What time?"

"As soon as we're ready to leave, he says. And he says we should bring Mick, too."

"That will be even more fun," said Bess, shooting Nancy a sidelong glance. "Won't it?"

Nancy hesitated, but just for a second. After all, Ned *had* passed up the chance to come along on this trip. Besides, she and Mick were just friends. Weren't they?

"It will *definitely* be more fun with Mick along," she decided. "I'll go call Franz right after breakfast to say we're coming. Maybe one of you could track down Mick?"

"I'll ask the concierge for his room number and give him a call," George offered. "And after I've totally confused her with my terrible French, we can try to dig out our bathing suits. I don't have any idea where I packed mine."

"Franz told me someone would be picking us up," Nancy said half an hour later as she, Bess, George, and Mick walked out of the hotel. "I don't see anyone here, though. I wonder if—"

"You are Miss Drew and friends?" interrupted a man with a German accent. Turning toward the street, Nancy saw a sleek limousine parked at the curb. "Monsieur Haussman sent me."

"A chauffeur!" Bess whispered as soon as they were all in the limousine. "I *knew* I shouldn't have brought that old Mickey Mouse towel with me."

Even Nancy couldn't help feeling awe a little later when the limo pulled into a long driveway lined with poplar trees. Ahead of them was a huge stucco house with gabled windows. The deep blue waters of Lake Geneva glittered behind the house.

"Wow," George commented. "I was expecting more of an A-frame or cabin, not a mansion. I thought you said this was a summer house, Nancy."

"It *is* their summer house," the chauffeur said as he pulled up to a graveled expanse on one side of the house. "The Haussmans have several estates. This one has been in the family for over two hundred years. Franz's father and his uncle and their families share it."

"It's certainly big enough for that," Mick said dryly. "Franz's uncle. Is he Erich Haussman's father?"

The chauffeur nodded. "Yes. Pascal Haussman."

"Oh, no," George groaned. "Are we going to have to watch Erich and Franz argue again? I'm on vacation!"

Both cousins were waiting for them at the

massive front door of the house, and Nancy was relieved that Erich was smiling as broadly as Franz. He seemed nothing like the tense and angry young man they'd met at Le Monde the night before.

"Hello!" Franz called. "Welcome to our— well, not-so-humble home. Come in!" He pulled open the front door and ushered them inside. "Would you like a tour of the house before we head down to the water?"

Everyone nodded. As he led them around, Nancy saw that the house was a spectacular blend of old and new. It was clear that every item in it was the best of its type. There were medieval tapestries in the drawing room, four-hundred-year-old tiles in the kitchen, and crystal vases filled with fresh flowers everywhere. Nancy had never seen anything like it.

"I'm afraid the second floor is too messy to show you today," Franz explained as he led the group back toward the drawing room. "I over-slept. Celine!" he called to a maid down the hall. "Would you bring us some *citrons pressés?* We'll be in the drawing room." In answer to Bess's puzzled look, he explained, "That's French lem-onade. You put in the sugar yourself."

When they were all settled in the drawing room with tall glasses of lemonade, Franz suddenly leaned forward and said, "There is an outdoor concert tonight. Why don't you all come? I wanted to make sure to invite you. A great rock band is playing—the only Swiss band that is any good, really. And the concert is being held out-doors at the Parc de la Grange, which you must see."

"Sounds like fun," said Nancy. "We can—"

"I see you have guests," broke in a man's gruff voice. "Would you like to introduce me?"

Startled, everyone turned to the drawing room doorway. Standing there was a thin, stern-looking man dressed in a gray suit and narrow striped tie. Behind his gold-rimmed glasses, his eyes had a cold glitter as he surveyed the group.

Erich jumped to his feet. *"Bonjour, Papa.* These are some new friends from America," he said, his voice cracking nervously. "And—and Australia. Mick is from Australia." Turning to Nancy and her friends, he stammered, "Th-this is my father, Pascal Haussman."

"And my uncle," Franz added. "My own parents are out of town."

"As we can deduce from the fact that neither you nor Erich is at work today," Pascal Haussman snapped. "Were you planning to go in to the office?"

"We don't need to go in today, Papa," said Erich, his voice strained. "We are working on a presentation at home."

"With your new friends?" Mr. Haussman asked, flicking a dubious glance at the group.

"Well, no," Franz replied. "We do keep flexible hours, you know."

"A bit *too* flexible," his uncle replied. "If you spent more time in the office, perhaps you wouldn't need to waste time—*and* embarrass your family—by getting into fights with men like Yves Petiau. That newspaper article was a disgrace."

"It won't happen again," Franz promised.

The sound Mr. Haussman made could only be called a snort. "Always so reliable," he said.

There was an awkward pause, and Bess leaped in to fill it. "Oh, he really is, you know," she gushed. "We just got here yesterday, and when we saw Franz at the airport, he just kind of helped—"

"The airport?" interrupted Pascal Haussman, his eyes narrowing. "What was Franz doing at the airport?"

Bess's eyes widened. "Why, he'd just come back from Monaco, and—"

This time Erich and Franz jumped into the conversation simultaneously.

"You know, the boat's waiting for us—" Franz began.

"We really should decide where to meet for that concert—" Erich said on top of his cousin's words.

They broke off and stared sheepishly at each other. Nancy was sure they had been trying to cut off Bess. But why?

Erich's father seemed to be wondering the same thing. He stared impassively at the two young men for a second, then turned and walked out of the room.

"Uh-oh," Bess said. "Did I put my foot in it somehow?"

"You could never do that," Franz told her gallantly. "Now let's all go down to the lake. I very much feel the need for some fresh air."

Nancy knew what he meant. Under the disapproving eye of Franz's uncle, the beautiful house suddenly turned unwelcoming.

She breathed a sigh of relief when they made their way out onto a large brick patio and then onto the lawn. They headed down a gentle slope toward the lake, which was filled with sailboats, speedboats, and dozens of swimmers on various beaches. A wooden dock jutted out into the water. Next to it was a charming flagstone terrace where guests could sit and enjoy the magnificent view. Nancy saw a row of white-painted wooden cabanas at the water's edge for changing.

"Wow!" George exclaimed, pointing to a slick white speedboat about twenty feet long that was moored to the dock. "That's a Sonata, isn't it? They can go, like, a million miles an hour!"

Erich chuckled. "Almost. Let's change, and you can see for yourself."

Franz, Erich, and Mick were already in the Sonata when the girls came out of the cabana. Erich was at the wheel, and he waved at the girls to hurry. "Let's go!" he called. "The water is perfect today!"

When the girls were sitting down—Nancy next to Mick, George next to Franz, and Bess up in front with Erich—Erich switched on the motor. The Sonata shot out into the water, and within seconds they had left the shore far behind. When they were so far out that Nancy could no longer see the Haussmans' dock, Erich switched off the motor. "Pretty powerful, huh?"

"It's a great boat," George agreed, leaning forward to trail her fingers in the clear water. "And the water feels good, too. I'm dying to go skiing."

Nancy laughed as she handed George a life preserver from under the seat. "The athlete in you calls. Why don't you go first?"

George vaulted over the side of the boat and quickly slipped on the skis Franz handed her. Then she grabbed the long towrope that was fastened to the rear of the boat. Mick watched her with an eager expression on his handsome face.

"I bet you want to get out there, too," Nancy guessed. She pointed to the second towrope that was affixed to the boat's stern. "Look—two people can ski at once. Why don't you hop in?"

She didn't have to ask twice. "Love to," Mick said, jumping up.

As the boat started up again, George and Mick broke into broad smiles. They were both expert skiers, and it was a pleasure to watch them as they cut steadily through the water. When they finally surrendered their skis to Nancy and Franz, Nancy joked, "You pros better not watch me while I'm out there. There's no way I can measure up to you."

Still, it felt great to be on water skis for the first time that summer—and to be in Geneva on top of it all. Nancy leaned back contentedly as spray foamed up into her face and the wind whipped her hair. This is perfect! she said to herself. She turned to her left to smile at Franz.

Suddenly she heard a deep hum that was even louder than the Sonata's motor. With no warning at all, a black cruiser cut in front of the Sonata with murderous speed.

"Hey!" Nancy heard Erich shout from his place at the steering wheel. Waves from the cruiser began to chop up the water around the Sonata, and Nancy had to struggle desperately to keep her balance. Out of the corner of her eye she could see Franz was having the same trouble.

Nancy gasped as Franz dropped the rope and fell face forward into the water. Before she had time to react, the Sonata veered abruptly, causing Nancy to lose her balance!

She screamed, but the deafening noise of the black cruiser drowned out the sound. Horrified, Nancy realized that the cruiser hadn't slowed down as it turned. Instead, it was going even faster than before. And it was heading straight for her and Franz!

Chapter

Five

NANCY TRIED TO TWIST to the right, out of the path of the cruiser, and fell into the water. When she surfaced, a wave hit her in the face, sending her under again. Choking and gasping, Nancy tried desperately to right herself.

Where was the boat? Which way was up? Where was Franz? The deadly roar of an engine told her the cruiser was on her, then the noise died abruptly and her life jacket buoyed her to the surface. Pushing her wet hair out of her eyes, Nancy saw the cruiser speeding away from them.

Horrified, Nancy realized that she couldn't see Franz anywhere. Panic coursed through her until she finally spotted him bobbing in the water on the far side of the Sonata.

Then there was a splash, and Mick was in the

water next to her. "You're all right," he murmured as he guided her toward the boat. Finally she and Franz were back aboard the Sonata, staring silently at their friends.

Mick broke the silence. "That wasn't an accident," he said grimly. "Whoever aimed that boat at you meant to hit you."

"Or maybe just to scare us," Nancy said in a shaky voice. She turned to Franz and asked, "Did you see who was driving that cruiser? It was on us so fast that I didn't notice."

Franz shook his head. "I saw nothing," he said. "When I realized what was about to happen, I just closed my eyes and waited for the end."

"None of you saw?" Nancy asked the others.

Erich bit his lip thoughtfully. "The Montreux have a cruiser, but I couldn't tell if that was it. I was watching you and Franz, not the boat."

Bess shuddered. "Can we go back to shore?" she asked.

"Of course," Erich agreed. "We've all suffered a shock. Let's go back at once."

They were silent during the ride back to the dock and were subdued as they changed into dry clothes. The festive mood of just a short time earlier was gone. It wasn't until a servant had brought a picnic lunch out to the dock that any of them could bring themselves to talk about what had happened.

"Franz, I can't help wondering if this has anything to do with that attack on you at Le Monde last night," Nancy said, making herself take a bit of bread and pâté, even though she wasn't hungry.

Erich spoke up quickly. "This has nothing to do with last night," he said firmly. "It was an isolated incident. And as for last night—well, people sometimes get a little crazy in clubs."

"A little crazy? That person threatened to kill Franz," Mick pointed out.

Franz shrugged uncomfortably. "Maybe I'm not so popular with some people—like Monique's parents." He poked his fork without enthusiasm at the bits of tuna and egg in the niçoise salad on his plate. "They think I'm being unfair to her just because I'm not ready to settle down yet."

"Do you really believe the Montreux would send a hit man after their own daughter's boyfriend?" Nancy asked.

Franz grimaced. "It does sound incredible, but I can't think who else it could be." He didn't quite meet her eyes, Nancy noticed. Was he holding something back?

"What about Yves Petiau?" George asked.

Both Franz and Erich whipped around to stare at her. "Yves Petiau? How do you know that name?" Franz snapped.

"Is it some kind of secret?" George asked. "We saw the article about you and him in the newspaper, that's all. Also your uncle mentioned him back at the house."

Franz let out a deep sigh. He and his cousin seemed to beam each other a warning signal.

"Forgive me," Franz said at last. He blew out a deep breath and rubbed his eyes tiredly. "I didn't mean to be rude." He jumped lightly to his feet. "And now, since none of us seem to have much appetite, how about a quick game of tennis? The courts are on the other side of the house."

"Here we are at last," George said in a relieved voice. "The Parc de la Grange. No thanks to you, Bess."

"Hey, it's not my fault I had the map upside down this afternoon!" Bess protested. "What do you think I am, an air-traffic controller?"

George chuckled. "Definitely not!"

After a quick game of tennis, Nancy, Bess, George, and Mick had said goodbye to the Haussman cousins and returned to their hotel. The three girls had attempted a bit of sightseeing, but the afternoon hadn't turned out the way they had expected. Instead of seeing the Old City, on the bustling Left Bank, they had somehow ended up at the city's central post office. They had barely had time to find their way back to the hotel and snatch a bite of supper before it was time to leave for the Parc de la Grange, where the outdoor concert was to be held.

"This place is great!" Nancy said as the girls and Mick walked toward the bandshell at the center of the park. They were just passing a huge rose garden with an eighteenth-century castle behind it. Dozens of picnickers were spread out on the grass. Some were teenagers in T-shirts and shorts who Nancy guessed were waiting for the concert.

"I sort of wish we'd thought to have dinner here," Nancy said to Mick, turning to look at him over her shoulder.

To her surprise, Mick was staring off in another direction. "Uh—yeah, I guess so," he said vaguely. "Very nice."

"Earth to Mick! Earth to Mick!" Nancy teased.

Mick blinked and stared down at her. "Sorry," he said. "I didn't mean to—" Suddenly he broke off. "Listen, Nancy, I don't think I'll be able to stay for this concert after all."

Nancy was completely perplexed—and disappointed as well. "Why not?" she asked.

"I—I have to meet someone," said Mick. His eyes kept veering off in other directions. "I'll see you tomorrow sometime, all right?" he asked abruptly. He walked rapidly away toward the rose garden before Nancy could say another word.

"What's eating *him?*" Bess asked, staring after Mick's back.

"Beats me," Nancy replied. "I think maybe he recognized someone, but I don't know who."

"Well, don't worry about it," Bess told her, scanning the crowd. "He'll be— Look! There's Franz!" She stood on tiptoe and waved.

Franz, Erich, Monique, and a girl with dark wavy hair were sitting on the grass about a hundred feet from the bandshell. They waved back as the three girls made their way over.

"This is my friend Claudia Beluggi," Monique said to the three girls. "We were at school in Zurich together. Nancy, Bess, and George are visiting from the U.S.," she explained to her friend.

Claudia smiled warmly at the three girls as she shook their hands. "I spent one year in the States myself," she said. Nancy noticed that her English was very good. "My father is a professor, and he was doing some research at the University of Chicago. Do you know Chicago?"

"Do we know it?" exclaimed George. "We're from right near there! Our town, River Heights, is only about an hour from Chicago!"

"That's incredible!" said Claudia. She giggled. "You know, I am from Italy, but I still dream about those deep-dish pizzas you can get in Chicago."

"They *are* great, aren't they?" Bess said proudly. "Still, I'm sure Italy has a lot of great stuff, too."

Claudia grinned at Bess. "It certainly does," she said. "In fact, you must be sure to visit me if you go to Rome."

"That's very nice of you," said Nancy. She exchanged a quick glance with Bess and George. "As a matter of fact, we *were* thinking about stopping in Rome. Our itinerary is pretty flexible."

"Then you must come!" Claudia said earnestly. "It would be such a pleasure for me! And I'm sure my family would—"

"Here's the band," Monique interrupted.

Three boys and a girl walked slowly onto the stage as the crowd sitting on the ground jumped to their feet and began cheering. Without any introduction, the members of the band picked up their instruments and began playing. They looked and sounded a lot like a heavy metal band Nancy listened to back in the States.

Although she wondered about Mick's odd disappearance, Nancy enjoyed the concert too much to think about him for long. The park was beautiful in the twilight, and it was fun hanging out with Swiss kids her own age.

Running into Franz at the airport really had been a stroke of luck, Nancy thought. She turned to smile at him, then did a double take when she saw his face.

Franz wasn't paying any attention to the music. Instead, he was staring at a piece of white paper in his hand, and there was no mistaking the expression of horror on his face.

"What's the matter?" Nancy whispered.

Franz shook his head. "It's nothing," he said. Frowning, he crumpled the paper in his fist, but not before Nancy had a chance to see what was printed on it. In large, block capitals the message said:

GIVE US THE TRUCK ROUTE. OR NEXT TIME WE WON'T MISS.

Chapter

Six

"FRANZ!" Nancy whispered urgently. "Who gave you that note? What truck route are they talking about?"

Franz started to reply, but the band started another song,..drowning him out. Nancy shrugged, then turned her attention to the concert again. Whatever news Franz had would have to wait until the band was finished.

Nancy couldn't concentrate on the music now, either. She was glad when the band was gone and the last cheers had died down.

"Wasn't that awesome?" Bess asked, her cheeks flushed.

"A little too awesome," Nancy commented dryly. "Threatening might be a better word."

Franz gave her a warning look, then got abruptly to his feet and pointed to an ice-cream vendor some distance away. "I am going to treat us all to ice cream from that man over there."

"Would you like me to come with you to help you carry?" Nancy offered. This might be just the chance they needed to talk.

"Oh—that is all right," said Franz quickly. "I can handle it."

Nancy wasn't about to let him off the hook so easily. "I insist."

Franz seemed about to protest further, but then he suddenly shrugged and grinned. "Yes, come, by all means, if it makes you happy. Erich, will you take care of everyone else?"

"With pleasure," said Erich. Nancy noticed that his eyes lingered on Monique for a moment.

The instant Franz and Nancy were out of earshot of the group, Franz said in an undertone, "I did not want Monique to know about the note. She is worried enough already. If she hears that someone slipped a threatening note into my pocket—"

"So someone put the note in your pocket?"

Franz nodded. "It must have happened while we were finding a place to sit down," he said. "It was crowded, and I remember someone bumping me. I did not see who it was."

"It sounds to me as if whoever tried to scare us on Lake Geneva is stepping up the threats," Nancy observed.

"I would have to agree with you." They had

reached the ice-cream vendor now, and Franz gave their orders in such rapid-fire French that Nancy only caught the word *vanille*.

"You are no doubt wondering about the reference to the truck route," Franz said soberly as the vendor starting making cones.

"Yes, of course I am." Nancy had a feeling that Franz was trying to decide how much he should confide in her. On a sudden impulse, she said, "Franz, I *am* a detective. I don't want to pry, but if there's any way I can help you, I'd be glad to. You've been so kind to us that I'd like to return the favor—if you can be honest with me."

Franz hesitated. Then he stared straight into Nancy's eyes and said, "Very well. I'll tell you what's been going on. But I warn you that it does not make me look very good."

Taking a deep breath, he began. "All right. You remember when I met you in the airport, I was on my way back from Monaco?" When Nancy nodded, he said, "Actually, Erich and I went together. Though he returned a day earlier than I did. We went gambling, but then I—" Franz broke off with a look of self-loathing.

Nancy tried to guess where this was leading. "You told us that the casinos had been good to you," she recalled.

"It was more complicated than that," he told her. "At first I did very well—so well that I began to take bigger and bigger risks. What a fool!" Franz exclaimed bitterly. "And, of course, that is when I began to lose. I spent the whole night at the tables, and in the morning I had lost everything I had started out with—and more."

"Pardon, monsieur," interrupted the ice-cream vendor. *"Vos glaces sont prêtes."*

For a second Franz stared blankly at the man. Then he fumbled in his pocket for his wallet, pulled out a bill without looking at it, and handed it over. With the same distracted air, Franz took the tray of ice-cream cones, and he and Nancy began walking back toward the others.

"So, anyway, it was dawn, and I was still at the tables—completely out of money. That was when Bart appeared."

Nancy raised her eyebrows. "Bart?"

"Bart," Franz repeated. "In a movie, he would play the part of the mysterious American."

An American, Nancy thought, and the threatening note had been in English. . . .

"Bart was very kind to me," Franz continued. "He offered to lend me some money—just to tide me over until I started winning again, he said. Well, what could I do? I can see in your eyes what you're thinking, Nancy—that I should have turned down the loan and stopped gambling then and there. Well, you're right."

Franz gave a short, mirthless laugh. He obviously felt awful about what he had done, and Nancy didn't have the heart to say anything to make him feel worse.

"But I didn't do the sensible thing," Franz

went on. "I took Bart's money and started to play again. I won back everything I had lost and more." He broke off and shook his head.

"So what was the problem?" Nancy asked.

"The problem was that I promised to repay Bart in Geneva. He called me the second I got home—I guess he must have been following me," Franz said darkly. "Anyway, he told me he didn't want me to repay him with money. Instead, he wanted me to do him a favor."

Franz stopped and soberly met Nancy's eyes. "He wanted me to help him steal a shipment of gold my father's company will be receiving on Friday."

"What!" Nancy gasped. "But that's only four days away! How did he know about the shipment?"

Franz shrugged. "He did not tell me."

Nancy's mind whirled, trying to make sense of this. "What's the gold for? Watches?"

"Exactement," Franz told her. "Frères Haussman has a line of top-quality gold pocket watches. We make very few of them. There is a waiting list several years long to buy one.

"The gold is delivered by truck," he went on, "but only once or twice a year. It is an important event for the company."

"So that's what the note meant when it mentioned the truck route," Nancy guessed. "The route the truck will take to deliver the gold?"

"Right," Franz confirmed with a nod. "Bart

wants the date and time of delivery, too. Naturally I said I would have nothing to do with such a plan."

Franz's face was flushed as he continued. "I—I may get a little carried away sometimes, but I would never betray my family. Well, as you might imagine Bart was not happy with my refusal. That is why he—he found me at Le Monde last night," Franz finished.

So that was who Franz's attacker had been! "I had a feeling you recognized him," Nancy said. "But why, when you knew who he was, did you accuse Monique's father of hiring him to hurt you?" Nancy was rather shocked by his actions at the club.

"I don't know. I just blurted it—I said anything so no one would know I knew Bart. It was rather cowardly of me, wasn't it?"

Nancy didn't voice her agreement. "Did you also recognize the driver of that black boat earlier today?" she asked instead.

Franz shook his head. "I never got a chance to see him!"

"Have you told the police about any of this?"

Franz snorted. "They would never believe me —not with my reputation." He shrugged helplessly.

"What about your parents?" Nancy asked.

"They're on vacation. Trekking in Nepal," Franz said bleakly. "My uncle Pascal is handling all of Papa's business affairs, and—well, you saw my uncle for yourself this morning."

Nancy smiled sympathetically. "I can see he's not a person you'd want to confide in. He doesn't seem to have a lot of faith in you."

"Not even at the best of times—and, Nancy, this is a very *bad* time. Last night Uncle Pascal told me that if I keep dragging the family into scandals, he will bar me from Frères Haussman. If he finds out about Bart or what happened in Monaco, I am sure he'll carry out his threat," Franz said earnestly. "Believe me, I love my work. I can't risk losing everything."

Franz started to say something else, then broke off and stared down at his hand. "The ice cream is starting to melt," he said, "and the others will wonder what has been keeping us."

As they began walking back toward their friends, Nancy asked, "You have no way of contacting Bart, I assume?" Franz shook his head. "Then how would you like it if I did some investigating for you?"

Franz's surprise showed on his face. "But you're on vacation! I couldn't ask——"

"I'd love to help," Nancy said, and she meant it. "If you promise no more lies." He nodded. "Now, let's see. We need to think about motive first of all. What about Yves Petiau or Monique's family? Could Bart be working for one of them?"

"There is a remote possibility, I suppose," Franz said reluctantly. "Petiau might want to steal our gold. And Monique's parents—well, they have their little problems with me."

Nancy nodded decisively. "Then that's where

I'll start investigating. It's too late to do anything tonight, though. Could I meet you somewhere tomorrow morning so you could tell me more about them?"

"There's a sidewalk café across the street from the Frères Haussman building," Franz suggested. Handing the tray of ice cream to Nancy, he pulled out a piece of paper and jotted down the address for her. "How's eleven o'clock?"

"Eleven o'clock it is," Nancy agreed.

As they approached their friends, carrying the now-dripping tray of ice-cream cones, Nancy's mind was hard at work. Would following up on the Montreux family or Yves Petiau yield any leads? If it didn't, where would the investigation proceed from there?

To Mick Devlin? a small voice inside Nancy whispered. Was it only a coincidence that Mick had turned up just when Nancy and her friends had become involved with Franz? What about his strange disappearance that night, just before Franz discovered the threatening note in his pocket?

Was Mick a suspect in this case? Nancy did her best to ignore that thought, but try as she might, she couldn't shut it out completely.

"No, Bess," George said firmly the next morning. "You are absolutely *not* buying a cuckoo clock. I would totally die of embarrassment."

"But cuckoo clocks are what people buy in Switzerland!" Bess protested. "As long as Franz isn't here yet, why can't I just run across the street and look in that store window?"

"Bess, we wouldn't be able to afford a postcard from one of these stores," Nancy said. "I'm not even sure we can afford this coffee we're drinking, come to think of it."

It was quarter after eleven. Nancy, Bess, and George were sitting at a sidewalk café on Geneva's rue du Rhône, a bustling street lined with very tempting—and expensive—shops. The night before, Nancy had filled Bess and George in on the story Franz had told her, and they had volunteered to help. The three had shown up at the sidewalk café promptly at eleven, but so far there was no sign of Franz. They had already finished their coffee, and now they were starting to get restless.

"I hope Franz hasn't forgotten to come," Bess fretted. "We have to meet Mick at twelve-thirty, don't forget. We can't wait here forever."

Mick had shown up at breakfast in the hotel's small restaurant and joined the girls for croissants and coffee. He hadn't offered any explanation of where he'd been the night before, but he'd asked the girls to visit the Cathédrale de Saint-Pierre with him. He had been so friendly and charming that Nancy had pushed all her doubts about him aside.

"Franz wouldn't forget. Not when he's in so much trouble," George was saying now. "Where do you think the Frères Haussman offices are, Nan?"

Nancy glanced quickly up and down the rue du Rhône. "Over there," she said, pointing across the street to a building whose bronze and glass facade managed to combine the best features of an elegant townhouse and a skyscraper. The first floor appeared to be a showroom for the company's watches.

"Looks pretty impressive," George observed. She squinted at the brass plaque next to one of the building's revolving doors. "Yes, you're right. That says Frères Haus—"

Suddenly George stiffened. "Nancy, look!" she whispered. "Over in that alley."

A small alley in deep shadow ran alongside the building. Stepping out of the shadows was a tall, bearded man, who stared furtively at the entrance to the Frères Haussman offices, before ducking back again.

"Hey, that guy looks awfully familiar," Bess said. "Where have I—"

"In the newspaper," Nancy said, jumping to her feet. "On the front page, being punched in the face by Franz. That's Yves Petiau!"

"What's he doing lurking around the Haussman building?" George wondered aloud.

"I don't know," Nancy replied, tossing some money on the table, "but I bet it's nothing good. Come on, we've got to talk to him!"

Chapter

Seven

"Don't let Petiau know we're following him," Nancy said in a low voice. "Pretend to be window-shopping and move closer gradually."

"Cuckoo clock window-shopping," Bess said. "The shop *is* right next to that alley."

As casually as possible, the girls crossed the street to the store window Bess had pointed out. Yves Petiau had no reason to suspect them, Nancy thought. He couldn't possibly know they knew who he was, nor that they suspected that he might be behind the threats to Franz.

"That's a nice clock," Bess spoke up in a bright, artificial voice. She pointed to a wooden clock high in the window—a gesture that let her turn toward Yves Petiau. "He's still there," she whispered to Nancy and George.

George rolled her eyes. "He won't be for long if you keep acting so weird," she muttered. "Tone down the drama a little, okay?"

"Oh—sorry." Blushing, Bess stared into the shop window. Suddenly Nancy realized that a mirror set in one corner of the window display gave her a strategic view of Yves Petiau. She bent forward and pretended to smooth her reddish blond hair in the mirror, keeping an eye on Petiau all the time.

As Nancy watched, Petiau checked his watch and stepped forward again. He seemed to be trying to spot something—or someone—inside the Frères Haussman showroom. Then he darted back into the shadows. Finally, after checking his watch, he started to leave.

"Come on," Nancy said quietly. "We've got to follow him and find out what he's up to."

"Monsieur Petiau!" she called out.

Startled, the tall, bearded man turned around.

Now what am I going to say? Nancy wondered frantically. She smoothed back her hair and smiled at Petiau. "I'm an American, and I couldn't help but notice your picture in the newspaper the other day," she said. "Do you really think your watches are better than the Haussman watches? Because I'd like to buy a watch to take home, and—"

"Of course mine are superior." Yves Petiau had the deepest voice Nancy had ever heard. "Haussman watches are overrated."

"You seemed awfully interested in the Haussman showroom just then," Nancy pointed out in an innocent voice. "Can you show me which of the watches in there is overrated—just so I'll know what to avoid?"

Petiau glowered at her. "I don't have time for this," he growled. Spinning on his heel, he stalked down the alley next to the showroom.

The girls followed as fast as they could. The narrow, cobbled alley led out onto a pretty street filled with tiny shops, sidewalk vendors, and cafés—but there was no sign of Petiau.

"I don't believe this," George groaned. "Where would he have gone?"

"There!" Bess cried, pointing. Petiau was walking briskly into a newspaper shop down the block. The girls followed as fast as they could, dodging passersby and stepping around the café tables. When they reached the newspaper shop, Petiau was no longer inside.

"The man who was just here—did you see which direction he went in?" Nancy asked the woman behind the counter.

"Pardon?" she asked, obviously bewildered.

Nancy realized that the woman spoke no English. She would have to try again in French. *"Le gentilhomme,"* she began carefully. *"Avez-vous—"*

"Le gentilhomme? The gentleman?" repeated the saleswoman. Smiling triumphantly, she reached down the counter to a stack of maga-

zines. With a flourish, she pulled one out and showed it to Nancy. It was a copy of *Gentleman's Style.*

"This isn't getting us anywhere," muttered Nancy under her breath. "Thank you very much," she told the saleswoman politely. "But we're looking for a real person, not a magazine." The woman smiled and nodded. Obviously she hadn't understood a word of what Nancy had said.

Back out on the sidewalk again, the girls paused uncertainly. On a narrow, twisty street like this, they might take off in twenty different directions with no guarantee of finding Petiau. He might be shopping; he might have caught a bus somewhere; he might be taking a stroll on the next block, for all they knew. In any case, he would probably refuse to talk to them any more.

"I hate to say it, guys," Nancy said with a sigh, "but I think we should give up. Anyway, we're due to meet Mick in a few minutes. I'll try to check Petiau out later. Maybe his address is in the phone book."

The Cathédrale de Saint-Pierre was located on Geneva's Grande Rue, only a few blocks uphill from the Haussman showroom. Bess read aloud from their guidebook as the girls walked along, and Nancy learned that the Grande Rue had just as distinguished a history as the cathedral itself. It was lined with impeccably preserved seventeenth- and eighteenth-century stone buildings.

"Hey!" Bess exclaimed as they passed one especially imposing baroque structure. "The Red Cross was founded here."

"And there's the cathedral." George pointed to an imposing building at the top of the hill.

As the girls approached the columned stone facade, Bess paused to look at it. "Let's see—my book says the inside of the nave was built in the twelfth century, and the front was built in the eighteenth century. The altar inside is Gothic, but the steeple was built at the beginning of *this* century—"

"And Mick's not around to hear any of this," George interrupted, glancing around them. "Boy, everyone's standing us up today. First no Franz, and now no Mick."

"Oh, well, at least it's a nice spot to wait," Nancy said. She walked to the stone steps leading up to the cathedral's entrance. "Let's park ourselves here for a while. Mick'll turn up."

It was nice sitting on the steps, anyway. Tour groups came and went, and the organ music floating out from inside the cathedral added its own charm to the scene. About twenty minutes had passed when Nancy's gaze lingered casually on a dark blue Mercedes that was drawing up to the cathedral.

Suddenly her blue eyes widened. "Hey, isn't that— Yes, it's Mick! Who's that driving him?"

A middle-aged man was in the driver's seat of the Mercedes. Nancy could see him speaking intently to Mick. Then both of them burst into laughter. Clapping the older man on the shoulder, Mick alighted from the passenger side of the car and closed the door. He gave the man an affectionate wave, then turned toward the cathedral as the car pulled away.

"Here we are, Mick!" Nancy called.

Mick's face lit up when he saw them. "Hi!" he said, loping up the steps toward them. "Been waiting long?"

"Just a few minutes," Nancy told him. "I didn't know you knew anyone in Geneva. Who was driving you?"

Mick's face went utterly blank. He looked away and cleared his throat. "Just—someone who gave me a ride," he mumbled. "The Swiss are nice to strangers, I guess."

To *strangers?* Nancy was positive that Mick knew the man in the car. Why was he trying to hide that fact now?

In the next instant Mick's expression lightened. Grabbing Nancy's hand, he pulled her toward the cathedral door. "Come on, you three," he said excitedly. "Let's climb one of the towers. You won't believe the view."

"Isn't it beautiful?" Mick said into Nancy's ear a few minutes later. They were standing in one of the cathedral's high towers, gazing down at the steeples and tiled, turreted roofs that made the city almost medieval. Bess and George must have wandered around to the other side of the tower,

Nancy suspected. At any rate, she didn't see them anywhere.

Mick laid an arm casually across Nancy's shoulders and pointed off toward the horizon. "You can almost see our hotel from here."

"Look at all the window boxes," Nancy said, marveling at the festive bursts of color that decorated so many of the old stone and stucco homes. Mick's closeness was making her heart race, but she tried to keep her voice light. "People love flowers here, don't they?"

"Genevans love everything beautiful. I wish I could swoop down and pick you a flower from one of those boxes, Nancy. I'd pin it right here." Mick touched her hair gently.

"Too dangerous," Nancy said with a nervous laugh, though she wasn't sure exactly what she meant.

"Bess? George? Where are you?" she called suddenly. "We should probably be getting back for lunch!" She turned to Mick. "Thanks for showing us the cathedral," she said in a voice that sounded too bright. "It's been one of the high points of the trip so far."

Once again Nancy wasn't quite sure what she meant, but she was definitely thinking more about the handsome, blond Australian next to her than about the view of Geneva.

Mick seemed to be perplexed, but he didn't say anything as they rejoined Bess and George and left the cathedral. They had a quick lunch and then found a bus stop down the street from their café. They didn't have long to wait before a double-decker bus pulled up in front of them.

"He really likes you, Nan," whispered Bess when the four of them had boarded the bus.

"Oh, I don't know about that," Nancy said uncomfortably. She was glad Mick was out of earshot, a few seats back.

"Well, *I* do. And I'm never wrong about these things," Bess insisted. "He's definitely gorgeous. Are you going to—you know—pursue the matter? I mean, what about Ned?"

Nancy sighed. What *about* Ned? After the way they'd parted, she had no idea where things stood with him. To Nancy's relief, the bus pulled up across the street from their hotel just then, so she didn't have to answer Bess's question.

The instant the girls and Mick alighted from the bus, Nancy saw Erich Haussman rush across the street toward them. "I've been waiting in your lobby for over an hour!" he said frantically. "Where have you *been?*"

"Just doing a little sightseeing," Nancy told him. "What's the matter, Erich?"

"The matter? The *matter?*" Erich took a deep breath. "The matter is that Franz has disappeared. I know something terrible has happened to him!"

Chapter

Eight

ERICH APPEARED more distraught than Nancy had ever seen him before. "Try to calm down," she said.

There was a small stone bench next to the front door of the hotel, and Nancy led Erich over to it. Bess, George, and Mick followed. Erich collapsed onto the bench and buried his head in his hands.

"I should have paid more attention," he mumbled. "That attack at the club—and the boat accident. Someone was sending Franz a message!"

Nancy was relieved that Erich finally recognized the seriousness of the situation. "When did you notice Franz was missing?" she asked.

"He went out after the concert last night and

didn't come back until after I was in bed," Erich told her, "if he came back at all. I never saw him this morning. I usually wake up earlier than Franz, so I was surprised when I passed his bedroom door and he wasn't there.

"I dressed and drove to the office," he continued. "Franz's office is next to mine, but he wasn't there, either. We were supposed to have had an important meeting with a client at ten o'clock, but Franz never showed up."

Bess glanced worriedly at Nancy. "And he was supposed to meet *us* at eleven this morning, but he didn't show up there, either," she blurted out.

"He was supposed to meet you?" Erich frowned. "He never mentioned that to me."

"I just wanted to ask him some questions about Geneva," Nancy put in quickly. Erich apparently didn't know about Bart's blackmailing his cousin, and she didn't want Franz getting into even more trouble with his family. "It was only going to take a few minutes. And, as Bess says, he never came. We wondered what had happened to him."

Erich rubbed his temples wearily. "I called home from my office. He wasn't there. I'm afraid he must be hurt somewhere. If I could only think what to do next," he said with a sigh. "My brain doesn't seem to be working today."

"I don't blame you," Nancy told him. "You've been under a lot of strain." She stared off into the distance for a minute, thinking. "Let's see, it seems to me that the first thing we should do is call Monique to see if she knows where he is. Then we'll check Franz's bedroom for clues."

"How did you get here, Erich? Did the chauffeur bring you?" Nancy asked after Erich told her he'd already checked with Monique's house. She was to be away for a couple of days.

"No. I took my own car."

"Then would you mind giving us a ride back to your house?"

For the first time that morning, a slight smile appeared on Erich's face. "Not at all. But I have to warn you—I drive a two-seater."

It was a tight squeeze fitting five people into Erich's tiny Porsche. When Erich pulled up to the house, everyone in the car sighed with relief. "My legs are asleep," George groaned. She had been providing a lap for Bess in the passenger seat, with Nancy and Mick crowded in behind.

Inside the house, Erich led them upstairs to Franz's bedroom. Nancy saw that the room had been decorated in a spare, ultramodern style, with black accessories, a chrome and leather bed frame, and a high-tech workout machine in one corner. But the room was so messy that the decor looked more rumpled than anything else.

"Franz must have left in a hurry," Nancy commented, eyeing the pulled-out drawers and open closet door.

Erich shook his head. "It is usually neater than this, but not much," he said. "Feel free to go through his things, if you want."

Franz's desk was littered with half-finished sketches and magazines—nothing too exciting. Crumpled in one corner, though, Nancy found a train schedule. "He marked all the trains to Zermatt," she said, handing the schedule to Erich. "Do you know if he was planning a trip there?"

Erich studied the train schedule with a puzzled frown. "Not that he mentioned. I'm sure he would have said something to me about it."

Looking over Erich's shoulder, Nancy scanned the schedule. "It takes four hours to get to Zermatt by train," she said, thinking aloud. "It's possible someone made another attack on Franz. Maybe he's on the run. I think we should head to Zermatt to search for him."

"I'm with you," Mick said gravely. "Should we catch the next plane out or rent a car? It might be faster than the train."

Nancy sighed. "I wish we could take a plane, but we haven't allowed for that in our budget."

"Besides, Zermatt doesn't allow cars within city limits," Erich added. "If we drive, we'd have to park miles away and take a shuttle bus in. We wouldn't end up saving any time."

"The train's fine with me," George said, and Bess nodded. "Me, too," said Mick.

"Erich, what about you?" Nancy asked. "Would you be able to leave work on such short notice? It would be great to have you come along, since we don't know Zermatt at all."

Erich knit his brow, thinking. "Yes, I suppose I could," he said at last. "There is a magazine there we might want to advertise in. I could check on it tomorrow."

"What's Zermatt like?" asked Bess. "What should we wear? Should we dress up? Are we going to spend the night there, or what?"

"Remember, guys, we can't really afford anything too expensive," George added.

"There are plenty of youth hostels in Zermatt," Erich said, smiling. "They're perfect for someone on a budget. I shall join you—it will be an unusual experience for me." Turning to Bess, he added, "You should bring any hiking clothes you have. We may end up doing some hiking or camping."

George's eyes lit up at the thought, but Bess was dismayed. "How will we ever carry our suitcases if we have to go hiking?" Bess asked.

"We're not bringing suitcases," Nancy said firmly. "We're going to take one small overnight bag, Bess. One bag for the *three* of us."

They just made the six o'clock train to Zermatt. It was comfortable and clean, but Nancy and her friends began to feel restless after three hours. By dusk their conversation had died out. After staring idly out the window for a while, Nancy decided to ask Erich a few questions that might help her better understand Franz's role at Frères Haussman. Perhaps Erich might tell her something about Franz's job that would illuminate a possible motive for Yves Petiau to attack him.

"You and Franz basically grew up in the family business, didn't you?" she asked. "Did you ever consider working somewhere else?"

"Oh, no. Well—I mean, of course I had ideas when I was younger, but my father knew I was best suited for the family business. It was a struggle for me then, but now I see that he was right."

Erich seemed so involved with the family business that it was a surprise to learn that he hadn't always been interested in it. "And Franz?"

"I don't think Franz has ever cared much for the business," Erich said, frowning slightly. "One day, you know, he and I will head the company. I hope he is as eager for that to happen as I am, or it will be an awful burden on him."

When Franz had spoken to her at the concert, he'd said that the company business *did* mean a lot to him, Nancy recalled. Now she wasn't sure what to believe.

"I see," she said, stifling a yawn. The compartment the five of them were riding in felt hot and airless. Across from her, Bess and George were already dozing in their seats. Mick was engrossed in a book. It was completely dark out now, and Nancy had no idea what town they were passing. It was only nine o'clock, and she was unwilling to give in to sleep so early.

"I think I'll stretch my legs a bit," she told Erich. "I could use some fresh air."

"Sounds good," he said. "I'd join you, but I feel too lazy. It has been a long day."

Mick glanced up from his book. "Want company?" he asked.

"No, it's okay." Nancy felt oddly shy about the idea of being alone with Mick again. Slipping out of the compartment, she stood in the hall for a second. There was an open window at one end of the car, she realized. That end of the car was empty, so she wouldn't be in anyone's way if she stood by the window for a while. Shaking the kinks out of her legs, she walked to the end of the car.

"Ah, that's better." Nancy breathed deeply, leaning her head out the window. The crisp Alpine air was refreshing on her hot face, and she loved the wind blowing through her hair.

The Alps hovered in the darkened view. They seemed so close that Nancy felt as if she could reach out the window and touch them. By the lights on the side of the train she could see that they were passing along a narrow gorge that dropped precipitously for several hundred feet. Nancy could just manage to see the jagged rocks at the bottom. She shivered. It was a pleasantly creepy feeling to be safe inside when the world rushing past outside was so forbidding.

Just think, she said to herself. A week ago about the most exciting thing that happened to me was ordering a pizza to go in River Heights. And now here we are in—

Suddenly Nancy heard footsteps coming swiftly toward her. Before she could turn to see who was approaching, two strong hands closed around her waist and hoisted her into the air. The next thing she knew, she was being pushed —hard—out the window.

Nancy's legs flew into the air. She struggled desperately to dislodge herself from the hands that were pushing her, but it was no use. Her stomach lurched sickeningly as she realized that she was already plunging headfirst toward the jagged rocks at the bottom of the gorge!

Chapter
Nine

Nancy's blood ran cold as she realized what was happening to her. Just as her body was about to slip past the confines of the window, she kicked out with both her feet and caught the sides of the window frame.

Her attacker must have already left her to her fate because he didn't push on Nancy's feet. She was left to dangle freely by her legs.

Nancy shot her right hand up and made a grab for the frame. In seconds she was seated on the window ledge, sweat streaming down her face, her knees knocking, and her heart thudding in her chest. She was safe though.

The train lurched beneath her, and Nancy exhaled shakily. She needed to get back to the compartment and sit down. Everyone else was sound asleep when she reached the doorway. Bess and George were curled up with their heads on the overnight bag between them, Mick slept with his head tipped back as if he were sunbathing, and Erich had a magazine balanced precariously against his chest.

As Nancy watched, the magazine slid off and thudded to the floor. The eyes of her friends fluttered open sleepily and came to rest on Nancy.

"Wh-what's the matter?" Bess asked groggily. "You look as though you've just seen a ghost."

"I hate to disturb you, guys, but I have to tell you something," Nancy said, sitting back down. Trying to sound as matter-of-fact as possible, she related what had just happened. When she had finished, there was an appalled silence in the compartment.

"Then that means that Bart could be on this train!" George said.

"Who's Bart?" Erich wanted to know as Mick slipped a comforting arm around Nancy's shoulders.

Nancy leaned back against his shoulder. "He's the man we believe is trying to hurt your cousin." Nancy had to explain the Bart incident in Monaco to Erich—she hoped Franz would forgive her.

"I can't seem to take this in." George looked as stunned and sick as Nancy felt. "How does Bart know who you are, Nan? How does he know you're investigating this for Franz?"

"I don't know," Nancy said soberly. She turned to Erich. "Maybe he recognized you, Erich. Maybe he decided to follow you onto the train, hoping that you'd lead him to Franz. Or maybe he planned to track Franz down himself and just happened to take the same train."

"Only how would he know where Franz is?" Mick objected. "We don't know he's in Zermatt. We're just guessing."

Nancy sighed. "That's true. All of this is guesswork so far. All I *know* is that someone on this train tried to kill me or warn me off this case. If that person is trying to find Franz, too—well, all I can say is that we'd better find him first."

When Nancy awoke Wednesday morning, she had no idea where she was. All she knew was that she was stiff, cold, and very uncomfortable.

Lifting her head slowly, she realized that the reason for her discomfort was that she was sleeping on a flimsy wood and canvas folding cot—just like every other girl in the room. Then she remembered where she was.

When their train had finally reached Zermatt at ten the previous night, Nancy and her friends had asked for directions to the youth hostel they had called from Geneva to hold space for them. Nancy had been so exhausted that she remembered little except being shown to the large, bare, dormitory-style room she now shared with Bess, George, and about twenty other girls. On one side of Nancy, Bess was sleeping; George was on the other side. Mick and Erich were off in the men's section on the other side of the building.

Nancy grinned to herself. This place made their hotel room in Geneva look like the Ritz! Not that they would be spending much time here. They had to start looking for Franz as soon as possible.

Reaching over, Nancy shook Bess gently by the shoulder. "Wake up, sleepyhead," she whispered. Bess groaned and mumbled something Nancy couldn't understand. "We've got a big day ahead of us. I'll wake up George—and then we'd better track down Erich and Mick."

"Have you thought about what our first step should be?" Erich asked Nancy while they ate bread and drank coffee in the barrackslike community room at the front of the hostel. "I am completely in your hands. I will do whatever you say."

"Me, too," said Mick. "Just give me a job."

"Well, since both of you speak French better than I do," Nancy said, "why don't you make a quick phone check of the hotels in Zermatt to see whether Franz is registered at any of them? There must be a couple of pay phones around here somewhere. In the meantime, we'll pack up our stuff."

Mick and Erich disappeared while the three girls brushed their teeth and packed. When they returned to the community room, the guys were waiting for them.

"Bad news," Mick said grimly. "Franz isn't registered at any of the Zermatt hotels—at least not under his own name."

"Great," George said, frowning. "We came here on a total wild-goose chase."

Erich held up a hand. "Wait a minute. Franz loves hiking, camping, that kind of thing," he said. "If he did come to Zermatt to escape, I think he would most likely be out climbing on Mont Cervin—what you call the Matterhorn. We could look for him there."

"Well," Mick put in, "it's a beautiful day to climb, even if we don't find Franz."

"Climb the Matterhorn?" Bess looked completely horrified. "What if we wind up in an avalanche or something?"

"It's summer," George reminded her cousin. "The snow is pretty much under control. And we can buy trail maps, can't we, Erich?"

With a nod he replied, "The mountain has trails for every kind of hiker. I have been here often before, so perhaps I should look for Franz on one of the difficult trails by myself," he suggested. "Nancy, you and Mick could pick out another route, and Bess and George could choose a third."

"A very *flat* route," Bess interjected.

George groaned. "My big chance to climb the Matterhorn, and I'll be doing it with the only person in the world who's allergic to heights!"

"Let's mark a few rendezvous spots on the

maps we get," Erich went on. "That way we can check up on each other every hour or so."

"Great," Bess grumbled. "That way an avalanche can wipe out all five of us at once."

"I can't help feeling as though I'm in a production of *The Sound of Music,*" Nancy commented to Mick a few minutes later.

Mick laughed, pausing to gaze down at the flower-covered fields and swift-running streams stretching out below the trail they'd chosen. "It does look like a stage set—or a picture postcard," he said.

The trail had been marked Moderately Easy on the map, but for the first few minutes it was rougher going than Nancy had expected. She and Mick had to climb single file along a rocky path before the trail widened.

Nancy raised her eyes and in the distance could see the snow-covered crags of other mountains. Far below the flower-filled meadows were neat squares of fields, looking like a doll's landscape.

"At first I was afraid I was going to have to spend the whole time looking at your back. Not that it's not a very nice back," he added with a smile, "but I'd still rather see your face."

"Isn't this a gorgeous view?" Nancy said, more to cover her confusion than anything else. This was the first time she'd been alone with Mick since the cathedral, and she felt self-conscious.

"It's perfect," Mick answered. For a moment

the two of them stared in silence at the majestic panorama below and around them. Then Mick slipped his arm around Nancy's shoulders and drew her close to him.

A little shiver ran through her at his touch. "We-we'd better get going," she said quickly, pulling away. "We've got a lot of ground to cover before we meet up with the—"

"Nancy, am I making you nervous?" Mick interrupted.

"Nervous? No! I mean, yes." Nancy could feel her face growing warm as she met Mick's gaze. "Yes, I—I guess you are."

"Why?" Mick asked. "I don't think of myself as being that terrifying."

"You're—you're not terrifying. In fact, it's kind of the opposite. I mean—well, what I mean is—" Nancy broke off. I can't believe what an idiot I sound like, she thought in agony.

"I think I know what you mean." Mick took a step closer. *"You're* kind of the opposite of terrifying, too."

Nancy couldn't help laughing.

"That's more like it," Mick said gently. He reached out and touched her cheek. "You don't have to be afraid of me," he said. "I'm not going to bite you. In fact"—he smiled—"it's kind of the opposite."

Mick bent his face closer to hers.

"Wait a minute," Nancy said breathlessly, her eyes still fixed on his. "There's something you should know. Back home, I have a—"

"We're not back home." Mick was almost whispering. "We're in the most beautiful spot in Switzerland. Together. Right now, that's all that matters."

He took her in his arms and covered her mouth with a kiss that made Nancy feel faint. Her whole body tingled with electric emotion as she leaned dizzily against Mick and kissed him back.

"Oh! Pardonnez-moi!"

It was a girl's voice, and it was coming from right behind them on the trail. Mick and Nancy sprang guiltily apart, turned around—and saw Monique Montreux staring at them.

"M-Monique!" It was hard for Nancy to put her thoughts in order. "What are you doing here?"

"Hiking, of course!" Monique was blushing. "I-I'm sorry I disturbed you." Then she shook her head. "But—what are *you* doing here?"

"We're looking for Mick—I mean Franz," Nancy corrected herself quickly. "Have you seen him?"

"But of course I have. He is here in Zermatt with me." Monique bit her lip. "In fact, until just a moment ago he was right here on the trail with me. But—but that was before our fight."

"Your fight?" Nancy repeated.

Monique's eyes filled with tears. "I have ruined everything," she blurted out, fumbling in her pocket for a handkerchief. "I brought Franz here to calm him down, and instead all I have done is upset him. What kind of girlfriend am I?"

What's going on? Nancy wondered. "Do you want to tell us about it?" she asked aloud.

"Franz has been so—so worried lately that I said we had to get away on a little vacation," Monique began. "He didn't want to go and leave work, but I insisted. I could tell he needed a break. His job is eating him dead—is that how you say it?"

Monique drew a quavering breath. "We have been camping here in Zermatt since yesterday morning. But then this morning we saw—we saw Bart on the trail ahead of us."

Bart! So he *was* here, just as they had thought! Nancy couldn't hold back a shudder at the thought. "Wait a minute—you knew about Bart."

"Knew about him?" Monique laughed bitterly. "My father *hired* him! Bart is a private investigator. He even has a temporary office in our house. My father was worried that Franz wasn't good enough to me, so he hired Bart to check up on Franz, but not to hurt him, of course. I still don't know why he attacked Franz at the club. I hated Papa's hiring him, but I knew Papa only thought he was doing what was best for me, so I went along with it. When we saw Bart on the trail, I blurted out to Franz who he was without meaning to."

For a second Nancy was too shocked to speak. It seemed hard to believe that Monique could so successfully have concealed her knowledge of Bart at the club when he attacked Franz. What else did Monique—or her family—have to hide? How did this all fit together? After Bart had been hired by Monique's family, did he decide to go off on his own to demand the gold shipment route? Or was he still acting for Monique's family? Nancy's head was swimming.

"I bet Franz didn't like your news much," Mick commented.

"To say the least," she answered. "I shouldn't have said anything, but I was so startled to see Bart that I didn't think."

Monique paused to wipe her eyes again. "So then Franz started shouting and said that Bart had been blackmailing him and trying to hurt him." Monique's dark eyes widened. "So Franz naturally thinks my parents put Bart up to this, but my father is not a criminal! He would never hire a blackmailer. I am sure if Bart *is* doing these awful things, it is not because my father asked him to. Now Franz will never trust me or my parents again! And how can I blame him?"

Monique's explanation sounded like the truth. No one could make up these connections, and Nancy was convinced that she believed what she said. That didn't clear Monique's parents, however. Could they really have hired so sleazy a character as Bart without realizing what he was like?

Nancy hesitated before asking her next question. "Monique, does your family have a big black speedboat?" she inquired.

"Why, yes, we do," Monique replied, perplexed. "What does that have to do with anything?"

Nancy explained that the speedboat that had nearly run over her and Franz had been black. She said no more, letting the implication of what she said speak for itself.

Just then Nancy thought of something else: With Bart on the mountain, Franz was still in danger. "Is Franz still on this trail?" she asked Monique.

"I—I don't know." Monique faltered. "He was angry and stormed off."

"I'll go look for him," Mick offered quickly.

Nancy nodded gratefully. "Monique and I will wait here," she said. "We won't move."

Mick strode along the trail in the direction Monique had come from. As the two girls watched him disappear, Monique said, "Now I have ruined your time alone with Mick, too."

"Oh, don't worry about that." The truth was, Nancy wasn't sure whether she was relieved or disappointed that Monique had interrupted her and Mick. "We have nothing serious going on," Nancy said. "At least, I don't *think* we—"

"There you are, Monique! I've been looking all over!" Franz's voice interrupted them. He came running down toward the two girls from a point above them and off the trail. He seemed puzzled to see Nancy but didn't ask any questions. Rushing up to Monique, he folded her in his arms.

"I took a shortcut so I could catch up with you," he panted. "I wanted to apologize for being such a fool. It was wrong of me to accuse your parents of trying to hurt me, but when I heard they had hired Bart, I just naturally assumed they wanted to—"

Suddenly there was a strange slithering sound. A handful of rocks and dirt skidded noisily down from an overhanging ledge and rained down on Franz and Monique. Startled, Nancy stepped back and looked up at the ledge—just in time to get hit in the face by another shower of dirt and pebbles. Coughing, she strained to see what was happening above them.

Then came an ominous rumble—almost like thunder. The next thing she knew, an immense boulder was hurtling down the hill toward them!

Chapter

Ten

WITHOUT CONSCIOUS THOUGHT, Nancy hurled herself at Franz and Monique. She caught them low and shoved them out of the way.

A split second later the boulder crashed past them, missing them by inches. Nancy actually felt the ground lurch beneath her feet. Another shower of dirt and rocks rained down from the ledge, and a bird screamed from somewhere up in the sky. Then all was quiet again.

"Wow." Nancy sat up and pushed the hair out of her eyes. "That was too close."

Monique gaped at the boulder now blocking their path. "That rock must be six feet across," she breathed. "How could an accident like this happen? These trails are very well maintained."

"Maybe it wasn't an accident," Franz said,

glancing nervously about him. "I bet someone pushed that boulder and meant to hit me with it!"

At that exact moment Mick came racing back down the trail. "I just saw a man on the ledge above you!" he gasped. "Then I heard—Are you all right?" he asked, pale with shock.

"Barely," Nancy replied. "What did the man you saw look like?"

"He was a big chap. Blond hair," Mick said. "Anyway, he took one look at me and took off."

"Oh, no," Monique whispered. "It was Bart! He really *is* trying to kill you, Franz. It's time I put a stop to this," she added. "I'm going to call my parents to tell them what's going on."

"I wouldn't do that just yet," Nancy said quickly. "It would only give Bart a chance to back off and cover his tracks."

"If he doesn't know we suspect him," Mick added, "we can catch him in the act—"

"And he'll go to jail," Nancy finished.

"But that means Franz will be a—what do you call it?—a decoy," Monique protested.

"I don't mind," Franz said staunchly. "Not if it helps us catch Bart."

Monique finally agreed to wait a few more days before speaking to her parents.

"Now, we should head over to our first rendezvous point and tell the others what's been going on."

"Fine," Franz agreed. He took a step up the trail, then paused to glance at Nancy curiously.

"Why don't you tell Monique and me why you're here? We didn't expect to find you on the mountain with us, you know."

"Well, when you stood up Bess and George and me at that café yesterday morning, we got curious—"

"Oh, my, I totally forgot our meeting when Monique called and suggested we get away. I am sorry," Franz said apologetically.

As the four of them inched around the boulder and made their way to the first rendezvous point, Nancy and Mick explained further why they had come after Franz. Before long, they reached Bess, George, and Erich. The three of them were delighted to see Franz safe and sound—and horrified when they heard how narrowly they all had escaped being killed.

"I *told* you this mountain wasn't safe. Let's get out of here!" Bess cried. "I think we should take the first train back to Geneva."

"Wait a minute." Now that he was out of danger, Franz suddenly seemed to have turned back into the cheerful, fun-loving person he had been when the girls first met him. "Why waste Zermatt? As long as we're here, let's enjoy it. How about some summer skiing?"

"Um, I don't see any snow, Franz," Nancy said, casting a skeptical eye over the green, mountainous terrain surrounding them.

Franz laughed. "There's snow at the top of the mountain," he explained. "People ski here year-round, you know. We can rent the equipment."

"Skiing the Matterhorn in June," George said, her brown eyes sparkling. "Kevin will die when I write him about *that.*"

"Let's do it!" Nancy said enthusiastically. "We may never have the chance again." At least they'd be relatively safe on the ski slopes, she thought. Bart couldn't possibly attack Franz in front of so many witnesses—could he?

A tram carried Nancy and her friends to the summer ski area high above the hiking trails. Nancy loved skiing, and flying down the slopes in hiking shorts and a T-shirt was exhilarating. The conditions were excellent, and the view was gorgeous.

So why am I feeling so dragged out? Nancy wondered as she stood at the top of the best slope she had ever seen. George whizzed by with a delighted wave, and Bess was eagerly alighting from the chair lift. Everyone else was in a great mood. So what was the matter with her?

Deep down Nancy knew what the answer was—she just didn't want to face it. The truth was, she was worried about Mick.

Not about their feelings for each other. Nancy was confident she could sort those out in time. What bothered her was that she was beginning to realize that Mick was not only a charming guy— but a possible suspect in this case. Maybe he was the mastermind directing Bart's attacks.

Everything about his behavior over the past few days was beginning to nag at Nancy. As she began a series of graceful curves down the mountainside, she made a mental list of all her suspicions.

To start with, Mick seemed to know more about Geneva than the average tourist. True, he claimed to have read his guidebooks carefully, but his familiarity with the city didn't seem as if it had come out of a book. Nancy was fairly sure Mick knew Geneva better than he was pretending to—but why would he lie about that?

Then there was the way Monique had recognized Mick at the club that first night. Had she perhaps spotted him with Bart somewhere? Mick had claimed not to recognize Bart on the mountain ledge, but he might have been making that up. . . .

Also, Mick had disappeared from the outdoor concert at the Parc de la Grange shortly before Franz had found the note about the gold shipment in his pocket. And he had shown up just *after* the huge boulder was shoved at Franz. In fact, Nancy realized, it was possible that he hadn't spotted Bart running away from the site at all. What if he'd pushed the boulder himself and blamed it on Bart?

What if Mick was Franz's attacker? What if he was just using Nancy to get at Franz? What if—

Suddenly Nancy realized that she'd reached the bottom of the slope. Wow, she thought to herself. I'm a better skier than I thought if I could negotiate that whole trail without paying any attention.

Still trying to get her thoughts about Mick into some kind of order, she skied smoothly toward the tram. Before she reached it, Erich whizzed up in front of her. "Wait! Don't go back up!" he said urgently. "I just remembered something."

"Something about the case?" Nancy asked.

He shook his head. "It's about my father. He is giving a party at the lake at seven tonight, and he's expecting Franz and me to attend."

"Oh, no. You're right," Franz groaned. He and Monique had just pulled up behind Nancy, with Bess and George alongside. "And it's already three-thirty! I've been so preoccupied that I totally forgot, too." Franz smacked his forehead. "How could I be so stupid? Uncle Pascal is angry enough at me already." He sighed and glanced at his watch. "Well, there's nothing we can do but leave immediately."

"But the train back to Geneva will take four hours," George objected. "And we still have to return our skis, collect our stuff, and get to the station. You'll be horribly late."

"We can't take the train, Franz," Erich put in. "We'll have to charter a plane." Looking over at Monique, he added, "Monique should come, too. I know her parents will be there."

George's jaw dropped. "Oh. I see. Well, a plane certainly *will* get you back in time."

"Yeah. Have fun at the party," Bess added wistfully. "We'll see you when we get back to Geneva."

Franz gave the girls a puzzled look. "What are

you talking about? You're coming back with us, of course. It's our treat."

"That's awfully kind of you," Nancy began, "but we really couldn't let you—"

"Nonsense," Franz broke in jovially. "You saved my life. Please let us do this one small thing. After all, the party won't be any fun without you. And Mick, too— Where *is* Mick?"

"Here I am," Mick called, skiing up to the group. "Hello, everyone. I hope you're talking about food. I'm starving!"

Everyone broke out laughing. "There is a slight change of plans, Mick," said Franz. "Maybe we can find you something to eat on the way to the airport. Now let's hurry, everyone!"

"Another limousine," George said a few hours later, pretending to be casual. "Summertime skiing, chartered planes, limousines—it's all getting a bit dull, don't you think?"

"Dream on," Bess said with a laugh. "It will never be dull to me."

Nancy, Bess, George, and Mick were riding in a limousine that Franz had sent to pick them up at the hotel and take them to the party at the Haussmans' estate. The afternoon had been pretty frantic. Nancy and her friends had raced to the ski lodge to return their equipment, raced to a private airstrip where Erich had chartered a plane, and raced back to their hotel once the plane had landed in Geneva.

They had showered and dressed in record

time—Nancy in an off-the-shoulder teal dress, Bess in a white jumpsuit, and George in an emerald green trapeze dress. Even Mick had managed to rent a black tuxedo. The only thing the four of them still hadn't had a chance to do was eat.

"I hope they have food at this party," Bess fretted, twisting her belt nervously.

"I'm sure they will," George said, peering out the limousine window as they pulled into the Haussmans' driveway. "Judging by the way they decorate, they probably know how to entertain."

The house certainly looked festive, Nancy thought. Every window was lit up, and a row of flaming torches led from the front door out to the lawn where the party was. Nancy could see a huge, white, torchlit tent on the lawn. There were people everywhere: sleek women in designer dresses, men in tuxedos, waiters scuttling around with trays of food and champagne.

"Come on, guys," Bess said eagerly. "Let's hit those hors d'oeuvres!"

As the group followed the torchlit path, Franz and Monique materialized at the edge of the crowd and came over to them.

"I'm so glad you're here!" Franz said warmly. "Now we can escape from all the boring old folks."

"And I would like to introduce you to my parents—not that they are old or boring," Monique said with a smile, smoothing the skirt of her dark red strapless dress. "They have heard all about you."

"They have?" Even to herself, Nancy sounded faintly alarmed.

"Oh, not that you are investigating these attacks on Franz," Monique reassured her quickly. "Just that you are new friends of ours. Mama and Papa are eager to meet you. Won't you come out to the tent with me?"

Everyone started to follow her except Franz. "I'll catch up with you later," he told them. "I need to check the lights out on the dock." He turned and stepped quickly across the lawn.

Monique sighed. "He just doesn't want to see my parents now that he knows they hired Bart," she said. "I can't really blame him. But when you meet my parents you will realize that they couldn't *possibly* have known what kind of person Bart is. They are good people, Nancy— really!"

Certainly Monique's parents seemed like good people when Nancy and her friends met them. Monsieur Montreux was a short, apple-shaped man with gray hair and a ready smile. His wife had once looked much like Monique, it was easy to see, but now her figure was matronly and her dark hair was mostly gray. The two of them hardly appeared to be the kind of people who would knowingly hire a blackmailer to terrorize a prospective son-in-law.

"We are very pleased to meet you," Madame

Montreux said warmly, shaking the hand of each girl in turn. "Monique has so much enjoyed getting to know you. Please feel free to call us if you need anything during your stay. Here is my husband's card." She pulled a card out of her purse, handed it to Nancy, and then turned to Mick, who was standing behind Nancy. "And you are—"

"Just Mick," he said brusquely. "No one important." To Nancy's surprise, he didn't even bother to step out of the shadows to shake Madame Montreux's hand. If Monique's mother was surprised at Mick's rudeness, she didn't show it. She smiled politely and then turned to greet a cluster of people who were passing by.

"What's the matter, Mick?" Nancy asked as they moved out of the Montreux' earshot. "You could have been a little nicer."

"Sorry, love," Mick said vaguely. "I guess they just weren't my type."

"Not your type? What are you talking about?"

"Forget it." Mick sounded as irritated as Nancy felt. Thinking back on the sizzling kiss they had shared earlier that day, she could hardly believe what was happening to them now.

"Just forget it," Mick repeated. "Look, I'm not in a great mood tonight, Nancy. I think I'll go down to the dock to see if Franz needs any help. As long as I'm stuck at this party, I might as well make myself useful."

With that, he strode off toward the water's edge, leaving Nancy staring after him.

"I wish I knew what's gotten into him," she said to Bess in a perplexed voice. "Do you have any idea?"

Before Bess could answer, there was a tremendous splash from the dock. For a second a hush fell over the entire party. Then Nancy heard Franz's water-choked cries mingled with Mick's voice shouting from the dock.

"It's Franz!" Nancy called hoarsely. "He's fallen into the lake!"

Chapter

Eleven

NANCY RACED TOWARD the water, feeling frightened for Franz. Her chest was heaving when she reached the dock and looked down at the water.

To her relief, she saw that George and Mick had already jumped in and were buoying Franz up. Within moments, they got to the dock's ladder and Nancy reached down to help Franz up. Mick and George quickly followed.

"Qu'est-ce qui s'est passé?" a stern voice spoke up from behind Nancy. It was Erich's father, Pascal. A waiter was with him, shining a flashlight on the three soaking-wet young people.

When Pascal saw Franz, he burst into a spate of angry French. Nancy couldn't understand the words, but she got the meaning without any trouble: Pascal Haussman was once again scolding his nephew for behaving irresponsibly.

Franz smiled weakly at his uncle and mumbled something in French. Then he gave a halfhearted wave to the guests who were staring at him from the lawn. "I'm fine," he called in both French and English. "Please, continue your party."

Casting one last angry look at Franz, Pascal Haussman walked back toward the house. The rest of the guests began talking, laughing, and eating just as they'd been doing before the accident.

"They're used to me," Franz said bitterly. "Old Franz, always clowning around. I'll probably have to die before it occurs to any of them that I might really be in trouble."

"You mean you *didn't* just fall in?" Nancy asked in a low voice.

"Exactly, Nancy. I—"

Just then Monique ran up onto the dock. "What happened?" She broke off as her gaze lit on the soaking wet trio before her. "Oh, but we must get you dry right away." Gesturing toward the cabanas at the edge of the water, she told George, "I'm sure there are some clothes in the women's cabana. Here, I will go with you. Franz, why don't you take Mick up to the house and lend him some of your clothes? You are about the same size, no?"

"Good idea," Franz agreed. As Mick began to follow the waiter up to the house, Franz turned to Nancy and said in a low tone, "While I was checking one of the lights on the dock, a man came up to me and slammed me against a mooring. He told me he would call me tomorrow at noon for the details of the truck route. He didn't even let me answer but just pushed me in the water."

Nancy's heart sank. Mick had been heading for the dock just before Franz was attacked! "You couldn't tell who it was?" she asked.

"No. The voice was muffled, and the person shoved me from behind. But I think it was Bart."

Franz followed Mick and the waiter to the house, and Nancy became lost in thought. She absently fingered the card Monique's mother had given her—then suddenly blinked.

Something Monique had mentioned in Zermatt flitted across her mind. Monique had said that Bart had an office at her parents' house. Since everyone connected with the case seemed to be at this party, now might be a good time to investigate Bart's office. He might have some files that would incriminate him, or Mick, or anyone else who might be in on the scheme to blackmail Franz. If all went smoothly, Nancy and her friends could get in and out of the Montreux house without anyone knowing they'd been there.

Nancy walked quickly across the lawn to Bess, who was talking animatedly to a handsome young man. She didn't notice Nancy until Nancy tapped her on the shoulder.

"Excuse me," Nancy said apologetically. "I hate to disturb you, but we have to go, Bess."

Bess opened her mouth to protest, but stopped when she saw Nancy's expression. "Sure, Nan," Bess said. "Let's go find George."

As the two girls headed across the lawn, George emerged from the ladies' cabana, dressed in navy slacks and a white polo shirt, both of which were slightly too big for her. "George!" Nancy called. "Over here!"

She quickly explained what Franz had told her about being pushed off the dock. "Franz thinks it was Bart, which means Bart may be at the party." Nancy couldn't bear to mention her doubts about Mick yet. "It occurred to me that this might be the perfect time to check Bart's office at the Montreux house. If *he's* at the party and Monique's parents are at the party—"

"Let's just hope their security system is at the party, too," George put in. "Because otherwise I don't see how we're going to get into their house in the middle of the night."

Nancy nodded thoughtfully. "I was wondering about that myself. We have to hope that the alarm won't be turned on," she said determinedly, "or that we can figure out a way to get around it."

"Aren't we even going to say goodbye to Franz or anyone?" Bess asked as the girls skirted the party crowd, heading back toward the house.

"We can't. I don't want anyone to notice us

going or find out where we're headed," Nancy said. "Why don't you go wait in front of the house? I'll call us a cab."

Twenty minutes later the taxi let the girls off in the quiet residential neighborhood where the Montreux lived. Nancy stared appraisingly at the large stucco building covered with ivy. It was dark and deserted except for a light burning in a room on the third floor. Nancy thought she could make out someone moving about behind the window shade.

"Someone's home," she said. "Maybe the alarm won't be on. And since they're way up on the third floor, hopefully the person won't hear us."

The three girls stole around to the back of the house to see if any windows had been left open. "Here's one," George whispered after a minute. "It's the dining room, I think. But how can we tell if the security system is working?"

Nancy peeked in over her friend's shoulder. She couldn't see any motion detector inside, and if there was one outside the house, it wasn't turned on because they would have set it off already.

Holding her breath, Nancy cautiously stuck a hand through the opening. Nothing happened. She reached her arm in farther, waved it around, and then gently tapped the windowsill. Still no sign of an alarm.

"I guess we just try climbing in very, very quietly," she whispered. "Boost me up, George."

In a second she had slithered in through the narrow opening. Then she peeked back out the window at her friends. "All clear, I think," she whispered.

"Whew!" George whispered back. "Give a girl a heart attack! I was sure the police would be here by now."

A moment later they were all safely inside the house. With Nancy in the lead, the girls began tiptoeing down the hall, trying to get their bearings. First they passed the living room, with its full-size grand piano gleaming at one end. The next room was a cozy little reading nook. After that, the girls came upon a paneled study.

"Wait a minute," Nancy whispered, stopping in the doorway of the study. The room held practical office furniture, one upholstered chair, and a file cabinet in the far corner. There were no paintings or pictures on the walls, and no signs of any personal possessions on the desk or worktable. Whoever used this room used it for business alone.

"This may be it. Let's check out that file cabinet," Nancy went on, stepping inside the study. While Bess stood guard at the door, George lifted a gooseneck lamp carefully off the desk and put it on the floor before turning it on. "The light won't show as much from the window," she whispered.

Meanwhile Nancy had quietly begun sliding open file drawers. The top drawer yielded nothing interesting. "Just some tax stuff, I think," she murmured. The second drawer contained accounts, the third what looked like copies of old letters. But in the bottom drawer, Nancy hit pay dirt.

"'Haussman,'" she whispered, pulling the file from the drawer. "Look, guys. They have a whole file on Franz!"

George peered over Nancy's shoulder as she leafed rapidly through the file. "Here's a credit check they ran on him," she said. "Looks okay, I'm glad to say. Some newspaper clippings, a press release about a design award he won—I guess he *does* take his job seriously—"

Nancy whistled as her gaze fell on a group of papers farther down in the file. "Okay—here we go. This is a report Bart made on Franz's activities."

The report was addressed to Monsieur Montreux and written in the form of a day-by-day journal. Surprisingly it was in English, so Nancy was able to skim it relatively quickly.

"'May 2. Subject spent all day at the office. Took a one-hour lunch at restaurant across the street,'" she read aloud.

"Thrilling stuff," George muttered sarcastically. "Do you get the feeling that Monique's family is wasting its money paying Bart?"

"'May 4. Party at the Lauriats'. Subject became boisterous and was asked to leave. Left without Monique, whom E.H. brought home later.'"

"That's still pretty tame," Bess whispered from the doorway.

Nancy had to agree. "'May 5,'" she kept reading. "'Subject late to work. Met Monique after hours—went to art gallery opening. E.H. confirmed art dealer a friend of subject's.'"

"E.H. again," Nancy mused. "Erich Haussman? But how could Bart talk to Erich without blowing his cover? We'll have to find out—" She flipped ahead in the report. "There's nothing much in May. Franz just got in trouble at a couple of parties."

"I think the Montreux should be ashamed of themselves," Bess put in. "Does it say anything about that time in Monaco?"

Nancy read ahead, then shook her head. "Nope. It doesn't even mention Franz's being there. Bart was covering his own tracks, I guess. He wouldn't want to leave any evidence about his blackmailing Franz. And I guess that means the Montreux don't have anything to do with the blackmailing. If they actually asked Bart to blackmail Franz, why would he bother to hide it from them in his report?"

Nancy leafed through the rest of the file, tremendously relieved to find nothing on Mick. "Look, here's a letter Monique's father wrote to Bart in April," she said after a few minutes' reading. "Hey, the Haussmans *recommended* Bart to Monique's parents! Listen to this!" Translating as she went along, she read:

" 'Monsieur Haussman spoke most highly of you to me. The Haussmans are as concerned as we about Franz's delay in committing to Monique. They have approved the somewhat unusual measure of hiring you to observe his activities for a short period.' "

"Somewhat unusual?" George snorted. "Yes, I'd have to say it's unusual to agree to have your son followed by a private investigator."

"Especially when he's a blackmailer," Nancy agreed wryly. "Though I guess these high-powered families do things a little differently from—"

Suddenly she stopped. "Listen!" she whispered. "Did you hear that?"

All three girls froze. "Someone's in the house!" Bess murmured in horror. She quickly closed the study door and hurried to her friends. "What are we going to do?"

Nancy could hear voices coming down the hall toward the study. Before she could move, the voices were right outside the door. Her eyes opened wide as the doorknob began to turn.

There was no time to hide. In a second they would be caught!

Chapter

Twelve

"QUI EST LÀ? Who's there?" a woman's frightened voice called out.

The doorknob stopped turning. "It's okay, Sophie," a man's voice said in a drawling American accent. "It's just me. Any calls for me?"

It was a maid checking on whoever had just arrived, Nancy realized. And just in time!

As the woman answered the man's question, Nancy slid Franz's file back into the file cabinet and closed the drawer. George was holding open a door next to the cabinet. Nancy joined her friends inside the small closet, and George pulled their door closed at the exact instant the study door opened.

Nancy's heart was pounding. Had whoever

was out there seen them? Had she dropped anything from the file on the floor? What about the light George had put on the floor—would the people in the study notice that?

It seemed an eternity before Nancy heard a voice, but when she did, she breathed a sigh of relief. Whoever was out there couldn't have spotted the three girls. He would never have asked the question he did if he knew he had listeners.

"No one saw us leave the party, did they?" asked the man with the American accent.

"I don't think so," a familiar voice replied. Nancy exchanged a shocked glance with Bess and George. It was Mick! "I don't think anyone saw you there in the first place, Bart."

Mick and Bart—together! Nancy's heart sank. This could have only bad implications.

"Well, what do you want to talk to me about, anyway?" Bart asked brusquely. "I don't want to waste any more time here than I have to."

"I want to make a deal with you."

"What kind of deal?" asked Bart.

"I know you have a lot of ambition, Bart," Mick said. "I can use my political connections—"

Political connections! Nancy was totally bewildered. What was Mick talking about?

"To, let's say, help you out with some of those ambitions."

There was a brief silence in the study. Then Bart asked, "So what's your deal?"

"What do you think?" Mick retorted. "I want money, that's all. I'm not very complicated."

"How do you know I've got money to give you?" Bart's voice was surly and suspicious.

"Let's just say I heard you were expecting to come into an . . . inheritance before long."

Was Mick talking about the gold delivery Bart was hoping to intercept? Nancy shivered. She couldn't believe it, but it actually sounded as if Mick wanted to get in on the scheme.

Bart snorted. "I don't know what you're talking about. Anyway, I don't need your help. Why should I ask for favors from a diplomat's kid when I've already got one of the most powerful people in Geneva behind me?"

Nancy's mind was reeling. Diplomat's kid? What was going on here?

"Maybe you do, and maybe you don't," Mick retorted. "The Montreux don't seem to be very powerful at dealing with their problems. Especially a problem named Franz Haussman."

"That little twerp isn't a problem," Bart said scornfully. "The Montreux don't have anything to worry about with him—not that I'm going to tell *them* that. I'm not talking about the Montreux. I'm talking about real power."

Mick gently pried. "I suppose you're not going to tell me who?"

"No way. But take it from me, someone a lot bigger than you is looking out for me."

"Well, keep my suggestion in mind," Mick said mildly.

"Uh-huh." Bart sounded utterly unconvinced. "Listen, I've got to get out of here. I just came back to get a little cash." There was the sound of his sliding open a desk drawer.

"I'll leave with you," Mick said. "I don't exactly want the Montreux finding me here."

The two men left the study, closing the door behind them. Nancy heard their footsteps fading away down the hall. Bess reached for the closet doorknob, but Nancy put a hand on her arm. "Five more minutes," she mouthed silently, pointing at her watch. She wanted to make absolutely sure Mick and Bart were gone before they came out of hiding.

The minutes ticked by agonizingly slowly, but at last the three girls tiptoed out into the study, made their way back to the dining room, and climbed back out the window to the deserted back lawn. For a long moment they simply stood in the cool night air, gulping huge breaths of relief.

"Let's get out of this neighborhood," Bess murmured. "I'll die if Monique sees us here."

It was a ten-minute walk before the girls reached a busy enough intersection to find a taxi. Once they were all safely inside the cab, Nancy gave their hotel's address, then leaned back against the seat.

"Whew! For a minute there, I really thought we were in trouble," she said.

"We really *were* in trouble," George said soberly. "We were just lucky, that's all."

"I can't believe Mick is such a—such a double-crossing jerk!" Bess added, shaking her head in disgust.

Nancy knew it was time to level with her friends. "I've had suspicions about him for a while," she said sadly. "Of course, none of the things I thought were true—but I was picking up on something." She briefly told Bess and George all the doubts about Mick that had surfaced over the previous few days. "But I was hoping he wasn't really bad," she finished, her voice trembling. She quickly wiped a single tear from one eye.

"Are you okay, Nan?" Bess asked anxiously. "I mean, you were starting to like him, weren't you?"

Nancy gave a wobbly smile. "I don't know. Maybe," she admitted. "I'm just glad I found out the truth about him before I really fell for him."

"Well, at least we know he wasn't working with Bart before tonight," George pointed out. "It sounded as though they barely knew each other."

"That's not much comfort," Nancy said bleakly. "He's obviously very interested in working with Bart, even if Bart said no."

Bess twisted a strand of her blond hair thoughtfully in her fingers. "Nan, could you figure out who Bart was talking about who was helping him?" she asked. "I mean, who was that powerful person he said was behind him?"

"And what was Mick talking about with that

diplomat's son stuff?" George added. "Is Mick's father a diplomat?"

"I have no answers to either of your questions," Nancy replied. "Yves Petiau may be the powerful person Bart meant. I haven't had a chance to follow up on him yet," she suddenly recalled. "We've been really busy since we lost him outside the Haussman building yesterday."

Nancy knit her brow in concentration. "I don't know about him, though. I mean, Petiau is rich, but I'm not sure he has the kind of clout Bart was talking about. Mick's being the son of a diplomat is certainly news to me. I guess I'll have to follow up on both those leads. Tomorrow," she added. The stress of their day—and her disappointment about Mick—had left her feeling drained and exhausted.

"L'Hôtel du Lac," the cab driver announced, stopping in front of their hotel.

Nancy fumbled in her purse for some money, but George was already paying the driver.

"Thanks for coming with me to the Montreux' tonight," Nancy told Bess and George as they unlocked the front door and walked into the deserted hotel lobby. The night porter was nowhere in sight, Nancy noticed. He'd probably gone off to sleep. "I'm glad you guys were there to keep me company in that closet."

"You know we wouldn't have missed it for anything," Bess said loyally. They rounded the darkened corner that led to the elevator and stairs. "If we hadn't been, I would never have believed—"

"Hang on a minute," Nancy whispered, freezing where she stood. "What was that noise?"

George darted a quick glance back over her shoulder. "What noise?"

"Someone's here," Nancy said tensely.

Just then, a dark form lurched out from behind a pillar, and a pair of strong hands grabbed Nancy by the shoulders.

Bess's scream echoed in the deserted lobby.

Chapter

Thirteen

Hey, hey, calm down! It's just me!"

Nancy couldn't believe her eyes. "Mick! What on earth are you trying to do?" she demanded furiously, yanking herself out of his grasp.

"I—I didn't mean to scare you," Mick stammered. "I just wanted to explain!"

"You've got a *lot* of explaining to do," said Nancy icily, crossing her arms over her chest.

George stepped forward and put an arm around Nancy's shoulders. "And attacking Nancy in a deserted lobby is a funny way to start."

"I'm sorry," said Mick. "It wasn't an attack, I swear! I just came down from trying to find you in your room, and I was startled to see you."

Nancy relaxed a little, but she was still determined not to let her guard down with Mick.

"Why don't you explain everything right here?" she said, gesturing toward a group of slightly threadbare chairs next to the check-in desk.

"Fine." Mick stalked across the room, flung himself into a chair. "I know you went to the Montreux house tonight," he said. "I saw you leaving the party, and I decided to follow you."

"Why?" Nancy asked.

Mick shrugged. "No reason except that I wasn't having that great a time. I hoped I could catch up with you, that's all. Then, when I realized your cab wasn't going to the hotel, I got curious and had my cab follow yours. I got out just as you were sneaking behind Monique's house."

"Hang on a sec," George said. "How did you know it was Monique's house?"

Looking a bit sheepish, Mick scuffed one toe across the floor. "Actually, I've been there before. I'll fill you in on that in a minute. Anyway, you went in, and I—well, I sort of hung back and waited to see what would happen."

"Right," Nancy said unemotionally. I'm not helping you out one bit, she said to herself.

"Then, all of the sudden, Bart drove up and parked across the street. I mean, I assumed it was Bart—it was the guy I saw up on the Matterhorn. I knew it wouldn't be good if he found you inside, so I decided to stall him."

He took a deep breath. "And the only way I could think of to get the interest of a guy like that was to offer to cut a deal with him."

"We heard you," said Nancy flatly. "We were in the closet in the study."

Mick's eyes widened. "I was wondering where you'd gone." He raked a hand through his blond hair. "Then I don't have to tell you what Bart and I talked about. I was making it all up on my side."

There was a long, ugly silence.

"I see you don't believe me." Mick's voice was disheartened. He slumped forward in his chair and stared at the ground. "Well, all I can say is, it's true. I was hoping that I could get him to incriminate himself somehow, but I guess he's too smart for that." With a sigh, he added, "I know it all sounds preposterous."

Nancy looked over at Bess and George. George's expression was guarded; Bess wore an imploring look, as though she was hoping Nancy would decide to give Mick another chance. Taking a deep breath, Nancy tried to decide what she thought about Mick's story.

"I *want* to believe you, Mick," she said slowly. "But I need you to explain a few more things first. What was Bart talking about when he said you were a diplomat's kid?"

Mick grimaced. "He was telling the truth," he admitted sheepishly. "My father was the Australian ambassador to Switzerland all during my teens. I—I didn't want you to know."

"But why?" Bess burst out. "Why wouldn't you want us to know a cool thing like that?"

116

"Cool?" Mick shook his head. "Oh, sure, you meet some interesting people. But I've always had to be on my best behavior. A diplomat's son—why, he represents his entire *nation!*" Mick's voice was charged with resentment. "That's the kind of thing I used to hear all the time. It's not always easy."

"Maybe not," Nancy said, "but your father isn't the ambassador any longer, so what's the problem with telling people now?"

Mick grimaced again. "I kept meaning to tell you, but it was fun having you think of me as just another traveler, so I kept putting it off. I know it sounds dopey."

"That older man we saw you with in front of the cathedral—" Nancy began.

"He's the current Australian ambassador," Mick explained. "We're old friends of his family. I saw him the other night at the outdoor concert and went over to talk. That's why I left so suddenly—I didn't want you to know what I was doing. We had breakfast the next day before he dropped me off at the cathedral. You can call him up and ask him to verify my story if you want."

Mick stared beseechingly at Nancy. "Am I forgiven? I know I should have been more up front with you. I'm sorry."

Nancy wanted to forgive him. Her instincts told her Mick was telling the truth. "I guess you get a second chance," she finally said.

Not that it will help this case at all, she thought

ruefully. She had no new leads. It was already Wednesday, and the gold shipment would be made on Friday, just two days away!

After the girls said good night to Mick, they headed up to their room. Nancy was quiet as she decided what was the next thing she should do. Talk to Yves Petiau again, she finally decided. She would try to talk to him first thing in the morning. All she needed was to think of a way to get in to see him.

Yves Petiau leaned back in the chair behind his massive desk at his office. He lit a cigar and stared at Nancy. "A reporter, you say? Which paper do you work for?"

"The *International Tribune*," Nancy replied. "I just started last year." She hurried on before Petiau could ask any more questions. "We're doing a feature on prominent Swiss businessmen."

Posing as a reporter had been the best way Nancy could think of to get in to see Yves Petiau. Leaving Bess and George to sleep in, she had called Petiau at his office just before nine. Somewhat to her surprise, he had agreed to see her right away.

"I have the feeling we've met before," the tall, bearded businessman said now, scrutinizing Nancy closely. "Have you been following me?"

Uh-oh. Now Nancy wished she hadn't spoken to him in that alley. "As a matter of fact I have," she said, trying to look suitably ashamed. "The other day, outside the Haussman showroom——"

"*Ah, oui!* That was where it was. But why did you not identify yourself then?"

"I was trying to get some background for my story," Nancy confessed. "I wasn't sure you'd want to discuss your rivalry with the Haussmans, and——"

"There is no rivalry!" snapped Petiau.

Nancy stared at him. This was certainly a surprise. "My—uh—editor's understanding was that you and Franz Haussman were very competitive."

"Then your editor was wrong." Petiau puffed ferociously on his cigar. "Let me set the record straight—is that how they say it in your country? We're going to be announcing it on Monday at a press conference, anyway. I don't expect you to print a word of what I say until then."

Nancy agreed and Petiau leaned forward over his desk and said, "Franz and I have mended our differences. We are the best of friends now. In fact, we are trying to work out the details of a collaboration between our two companies."

He scrabbled through the pile of papers on his desk, finally plucking one from the bottom of the pile. "There," he said, thrusting the paper at Nancy. "Can you read French? Then take a look at this, and you'll see that I'm telling the truth."

Nancy scanned the piece of paper, trying to translate mentally as she went along. She couldn't understand all of it, but she got the general drift. It was a letter Franz had written stating his intent to work with Petiau to develop a line of moderately priced, high-fashion watches for the younger market. From what Nancy could understand, Franz would be responsible for the design, and Petiau's company would manufacture the watches.

When she finished reading, Nancy's head was spinning. She was more confused than ever. If this was true—and she could think of no reason why it wouldn't be—why hadn't Franz mentioned the collaboration to her? Why had he allowed her to think that he and Petiau were still bitter rivals?

She would certainly ask Franz for an explanation, but there was something else still nagging at her. "Monsieur Petiau, what *were* you doing outside the Haussman showroom when I saw you?" she asked.

"I wasn't sneaking around, if that's what you're suggesting," Petiau snapped, tugging at his beard. "I had had an appointment with Franz that morning, and he hadn't shown up." Because he had been in Zermatt, Nancy knew now. "I was unable to reach him at his office, so I was trying to see if he was in the showroom, without attracting notice," Petiau continued. He gave Nancy a thin, reluctant smile. "I see I was not successful."

Remembering her cover, Nancy continued to ask Yves Petiau questions a reporter might ask. She nodded professionally as she jotted down his answers, but she was paying hardly any attention to the conversation. What was really occupying her mind was the fact that she was further from solving the case than ever.

It was Thursday. The shipment of gold was due to be delivered the next day, and Nancy still didn't have the slightest idea whether it would get there safely!

Chapter

Fourteen

"WELL, NAN? What happened?" George asked expectantly as Nancy walked into the girls' hotel room.

"Did you find out anything else about the blackmailing?" Bess wanted to know.

Nancy sank down onto her bed with a sigh. "Not exactly," she said. "This case seems to be turning up nothing but dead ends." Quickly she described her meeting with Petiau.

"I don't get it," George said. "That picture in the paper—I thought Franz hated Yves Petiau. What's he doing going into business with him?"

"Beats me," said Nancy. "But I doubt Petiau would blackmail Franz if they're working together. Still, I'd like to ask Franz about it. Maybe we could go see him at his office. I'll run down to the lobby and call."

In a few minutes she was back. "Franz's secretary said he's working at home today, so I called him there. He said it would be fine for us to come over now."

Franz was waiting in the drawing room of the Haussmans' summer estate when the three girls got there. "You sounded upset on the telephone, Nancy," he said after they'd sat down. "Is something the matter? I mean, is something *new* the matter?"

"I spoke with Yves Petiau in his office this morning," Nancy told him. "Are you really going into business with him, Franz?"

Franz grimaced. "So it's out," he said. "I wanted to keep it a secret until we announced it officially on Monday. I wanted to surprise my family, but if Yves is already telling people—"

"I don't think he's told anyone besides me."

"Well, why did he tell you?" Franz was clearly puzzled.

"He thought I was a reporter," Nancy said. "I guess he wanted to get the ball rolling, though he did say I couldn't print the story until after you'd made the announcement."

"Then I'm glad you're not a real reporter," Franz said swiftly, "because you *would* print it. I can see that Yves and I will have to formalize a few more aspects of our partnership—like who is in charge of publicity."

Nancy watched Franz closely. "So there's no way this deal could have anything to do with the threats you've been receiving," she asked.

"Definitely not," he confirmed. "It means only good things for me *and* for Frères Haussman. We have been looking for a way to break into the younger market, and I think this is it. Besides," he added, "Petiau was not fun to have as an enemy. It will be better for him to be on our side."

"How did you get him on your side?" George inquired. "I would have thought that you two were—uh—permanently incompatible."

Franz gave a sudden laugh. "It was simple. I realized that I should not have insulted him to such a degree when we had that fight you read of. So early Monday morning I sent him a letter of apology. He called me then just before you came to go waterskiing. Well, one thing led to another and I sent him a letter of intent to do business with him late that afternoon, before the concert. He called back again and the whole transaction was almost completed on Monday."

"Then why did you say Petiau might want to steal your gold that night?" Nancy asked.

"I still didn't know the man very well and couldn't really trust him."

His hazel eyes grew more serious as he added, "I hope that at last my family will realize that I have our company's best interests at heart. And maybe Monique's parents will take me seriously."

"Speaking of Monique's parents," Nancy said, "we learned something at their house last night."

"Monique's house? What were you doing there?"

While Nancy, Bess, and George summarized their adventure for Franz, Nancy noticed that his expression grew more and more shaken. She felt badly about bringing him such upsetting news, but she needed everything out in the open if there was any chance of solving this case.

"And you say my own family approved of their hiring Bart?" Franz asked when they were done. "I—I can't believe my parents would stoop so low! I will have to talk to them when they get home."

"In the meantime, can't you go to your uncle about all this?" Bess spoke up. *"Someone* in your family should know what kind of person Bart is—and how dangerous he is. We've got to stop him before the gold is delivered tomorrow!"

"Absolutely," Franz said gravely. "Uncle Pascal is out of the country on business, unfortunately. He won't return until tomorrow, when the gold is due. By then it would be too late to do anything!"

Nancy jumped to her feet and began pacing the length of the drawing room, thinking aloud as she walked. "Okay. So we can't get to your uncle," she said rapidly. "Then it's up to us. *We're* going to have to stop that heist ourselves."

"How?" Bess asked blankly. "We don't know the route the delivery truck is going to take."

"Or when it's making the delivery," George added. "Come to think of it, neither does Bart or the person he's working with. That's what all this fuss is about, remember?"

Nancy paused to gaze at her friends. "I certainly do," she said. "Well, I guess if Pascal Haussman is out of the country, we need to find out about the shipment ourselves."

"I doubt we'll be able to, though," Franz said gloomily. "My uncle keeps that information very secret. He would never trust me with it."

"Well, he's not here now," Nancy pointed out, "and this is an emergency. I'm sure he wouldn't mind if we tried to find out the truck route."

Franz studied Nancy thoughtfully. "Uncle Pascal *does* have an office here. It's upstairs," he said, rising to his feet.

Pascal Haussman's office looked just like Pascal Haussman himself—stern, correct, and unwelcoming. Rows of books were perfectly aligned in the bookshelves, and the papers on the marble-topped desk were lined up precisely.

"Let's try the desk first," Nancy suggested. "But, everyone, put things back *exactly* the way they were. Pascal strikes me as the kind of man who'd notice if a single paper was out of place."

Gingerly Bess, George, and Franz began leafing through the papers on top of the desk while Nancy opened the desk drawers one at a time. Except for the rustling of papers, there was silence in the room.

As Nancy pulled open the middle desk drawer, a manila folder on top caught her eye. "Delivery" was written boldly across the top of the folder.

It can't be this easy, she thought as she opened the folder. But it was.

"Route de Camion," said the single sheet of paper inside the folder. Under the title was a map and a list of times and street locations.

"Franz, doesn't this mean 'truck route'?" Nancy asked, handing the folder across the desk to him.

Franz's eyes widened in astonishment. "Yes," he said in a dazed voice, staring down at the sheet. "This is what we've been looking for! It is the route for tomorrow's gold shipment."

Bess and George put down their papers and quickly came to Franz's side.

"Translate everything for me," Bess begged. "I can't stand not knowing what it says!"

"It says the truck will leave at three in the afternoon tomorrow," Franz told her. "And that it's leaving from the Schlossinger Gold Company."

"Well, what does *that* mean?" Bess was practically dancing up and down with impatience.

"Schlossinger's is in the Old City," Franz explained. "That's not far from the Haussman offices. And this map describes the route the truck will take. We shouldn't have much trouble intercepting it."

"So our problem's solved," Bess said brightly.

"All Franz has to do is tell Bart the route, and then we can follow the truck, and we'll catch Bart when he tries to steal the gold!"

Then Bess paused, eyeing Nancy uneasily. "Why don't you look happy, Nan? This is good news, isn't it?"

"I'm not sure," Nancy said slowly. "Something seems wrong to me. It's all too easy. Why would your uncle put this route where *anyone* could find it, Franz? You just told us that he keeps this kind of information very secret."

"That's right." Now Franz sounded thoughtful. "Come to think of it, he has even been dropping hints about this folder to me. Just before he left, he told me to be sure to keep out of his desk while he was gone. Why did he call attention to the desk that way?"

George nodded. "Especially *your* attention," she said. "After all, he doesn't approve of you, right? You'd hardly expect him to go out of his way to tempt you."

"Do you think he wanted me to know the route?" Franz asked, bewildered. "It seems he did—but why?"

The four of them stared at one another in silence. "Well, I'm stumped," George finally said.

"I wish your uncle hadn't left town, Franz," Nancy burst out, frustrated. "It would be so much easier if we could just talk to him."

"I suppose I am an orphan for the time being,"

said Franz, shaking his head. "My parents have been away for so long. How am I going to explain all this to them when they get back?"

"How long have they been gone?" George asked.

"Three months. They have another month left."

"Wait a minute," Nancy said suddenly. "That reminds me of something else. That letter in Monsieur Montreux's file—the one to Bart—said your family had recommended him highly. But it was written in late April, and your parents were out of the country then, right?"

Franz nodded. "Right. So that means—"

"That your father couldn't have made the recommendation," Nancy finished.

"This is too confusing!" Bess wailed. "What does Franz's parents' being out of the country have to do with anything?"

Nancy tried to put her thoughts in order. "It means that Pascal made the decision on his own, which makes me wonder even more about what he's up to. What if—I know this sounds unbelievable, but could your uncle *want* you to get into trouble by finding this truck route, Franz?"

Nancy continued. "If he wants to hurt you, he might purposely have recommended that the Montreux hire Bart. Then no suspicion would fall on him when Bart started threatening Franz."

"I don't know, Nan," Bess spoke up. "That

seems pretty far out. Besides, we still can't be sure that Franz's parents didn't help make the decision to hire Bart before they left."

"But I'm sure they did not," Franz said firmly. "I know my parents. They don't like everything I do, but they'd never hurt me."

Franz hesitated for a moment. "But Uncle Pascal? He just might do something like that."

Nancy had been sitting behind the desk, but now she jumped up. "As long as we're here, let's check the rest of the office. There just might be something your uncle *doesn't* want anyone to find—something that could help us understand him a little better."

This time it wasn't as easy. A search of the desk didn't turn up anything more, and the tall oak file cabinet next to the desk was locked.

"I'll just have to pick it," Nancy said matter-of-factly.

Franz watched in awe as Nancy pulled a slender metal instrument from her purse and deftly began to work on the lock. "Is this what they call Yankee ingenuity?" he asked.

"Oh, Americans learn this kind of thing in kindergarten," George joked.

"That's right," Nancy said as she fiddled with the lock. "Reading, writing, lock-picking . . ." With a grin, she pulled out her lock pick and slid the top drawer open.

Inside was a pile of letters. "I think this is it, Franz," Nancy said quietly. "This is to Bart Jackson from Pascal Haussman." Her heart began beating faster as she lifted the pile of letters carefully out of the drawer.

"They're in English!" Bess remarked, looking over Nancy's shoulder. "But I guess that makes sense, since Bart's American."

Still, the letters were so cryptic that they weren't easy to understand. "'The target will no doubt offer some resistance initially,'" Nancy read aloud in a puzzled voice. "The target? How can a target offer anything? He must mean a person. Here he mentions the target again," Nancy went on. "'Once you have secured the target, the event will unfold without difficulty.'"

"What event?" Bess asked. "You're losing me."

Nancy shook her head. "'Your part in the event will not be taxing,'" she continued, trying to make sense of the ambiguous language. "'Make sure to leave the scene once the target is clearly involved with unloading the delivery. I will alert the authorities meanwhile, and it will be a simple matter to convince them of the target's guilt.'"

"'The target's guilt,'" George repeated. "This is so weird, Nan! What on earth is he—"

"Wait a minute! I know what he's talking about!" Nancy burst out excitedly. *You're* the target, Franz, and the 'event' is the gold delivery. You're supposed to get caught stealing the shipment!

"Pascal didn't hire Bart to watch over you," Nancy went on. *He hired him to set you up!*

Chapter

Fifteen

"THAT'S IMPOSSIBLE, NANCY." Franz's face was so pale that Nancy was afraid he was going to pass out. "My uncle doesn't like me, but he would never set me up. Not his own nephew!"

Bess and George looked just as surprised as Franz. "This is too much," Bess murmured.

"I know this is a shock," Nancy told Franz gently. "But what else could the letters mean? Why else would your uncle practically shove the truck route in your face when he's usually so secretive? Look here—" She pointed to a line in one of the letters. "Pascal gives a date for the 'event,' and it's tomorrow. It *must* be the gold shipment."

Franz read the letter in silence. His hands were shaking, Nancy noticed. "I—I see that you're probably right. And suddenly I see something else, too," he added soberly. "My cousin Erich must be involved in this. It was Erich who introduced me to Bart."

"Erich introduced you? In Monaco?" Nancy asked. "You didn't mention that before." Suddenly the references to "E.H." in Bart's correspondence made sense. Thinking back on Erich's bitter comments about Franz's work, Nancy had to admit that he had a motive for wanting Franz out of the way.

Franz collapsed into a chair next to Pascal's desk. "This is worse than anything I imagined," he said, groaning. "It was bad enough that Monique's parents didn't trust me, but my own uncle? My cousin who grew up with me?"

"It's sickening," Nancy agreed. "The letters make it clear that Pascal planned for you to be caught red-handed stealing the gold. The only thing he didn't count on was that you might have the guts *not* to cooperate with Bart."

George had been silent, but now she spoke up. "I know you're right, Nan. But those letters are so vague. We can't use them as proof, can we?"

Nancy frowned. "No, we can't. Good point, George. The police would never follow up on this." She bit her lip for a second, thinking. "I'm just going to have to come up with a plan," she said at last. "A plan to trap the trappers."

As if on cue, the telephone rang—but none of them made a move to pick it up.

"That will be Bart," Franz said, letting out a

sigh. "When I was pushed into the lake last night, he said he would call at noon today."

The telephone was still jangling. "Why don't you pick it up, Franz?" Nancy suddenly suggested. "I think we can improvise an answer to Bart. Sound happy when you answer, okay?"

Franz looked puzzled but did as she asked. "Hello? Bart! I was just thinking about you!"

That was certainly true, Nancy thought. She scribbled a message on a sheet of paper and shoved it across the desk to Franz. "Play along," it said.

Franz raised his eyebrows inquiringly at her, and Nancy realized he probably didn't know what the expression meant. "Tell him you'll cooperate!" she whispered frantically.

Franz nodded and began speaking again. "The reason I was thinking about you is that I realized I have been foolish," he said, winking broadly at the three girls. "I can see it would really be in my own best interests to cooperate with you."

Nancy grinned and gave him a thumbs-up sign.

"To play along—is that how you Americans put it?" Franz went on to Nancy's horror.

"No, no!" she whispered, shaking her head.

"I mean, to join in with your plan," Franz corrected himself hurriedly. "I have the route for you, Bart. I only hope I am not too late."

For a minute he listened intently to Bart. "Oh, really?" he said. "But of course I'm not trying to— No, no, I understand. . . . You're absolutely right. . . . Fine. We will meet tomorrow at three o'clock, outside Schlossinger's.

"And Bart?" Franz continued. "Thank you."

He hung up and turned to the three girls. "I think he believed me, but I'm not sure," he reported. "He says he's worried that I will double-cross him. So he wants me to ride with him during the heist. What do you think, Nancy?"

"I think that proves that he's setting you up," Nancy said immediately. "And I think you'd better—uh—play along. Just don't *tell* him that's what you're doing, please."

Franz nodded sheepishly. "I'll do whatever you tell me," he said. "But does this mean Bart will get to keep the gold?" he added worriedly.

"No way," Nancy assured him. "Instead of finding the gold, he's going to find *me.*"

Her friends stared blankly at her.

"I've just been working this out for myself," she said. "I think your uncle's going to call in—anonymously, I assume—to give the police a 'tip' about the gold heist. The police will arrest you when you and Bart try to make the heist."

George nodded. "So where do we fit in, Nan?"

"Now that we know what Pascal is planning, we can make sure it doesn't happen. We don't have much time," Nancy went on. "Let's start working on our plan for tomorrow. May I use the phone, Franz? I need to call Mick."

"Why?" asked Bess in surprise.

"Mick is going to be part of the plan," Nancy replied. "As long as he agrees, I mean. And somehow I have a feeling he will."

At nine o'clock the next morning, Franz headed over to the Schlossinger Gold Company in one of the gold company's limousines. With Nancy at his side—posing as his American associate—he asked the Schlossinger official he was meeting to delay the shipment of gold by one day.

Nancy could just manage to follow what Franz and the official, Monsieur Balch, were talking about.

"Why this change, Monsieur Haussman?" Mr. Balch wanted to know. He stared at Franz with obvious concern.

Nancy and Franz had prepared for that question. "We seem to have a slight problem with our computerized security system," Franz said now. "I didn't want to speak to you over the phone in case someone heard me. It's nothing serious, I'm glad to say—just a glitch in the back-up. But of course you understand, Frères Haussman can't take even the slightest risk with so much at stake."

"Of course, monsieur," the Schlossinger official agreed immediately. "We will be glad to delay the shipment. Is there anything else I can do for you?"

"As a matter of fact, there is," Franz told him. "I would like you to send along an *empty* truck at the scheduled time. Even though we are not receiving our regular delivery today, we would like to stick to our routine as much as possible. In case people are watching us," he added vaguely.

Now Mr. Balch sounded completely befuddled. "Excuse me? Watching you?"

"Naturally we wouldn't want people to think that we had altered our plans," Franz huffed.

Nancy had coached Franz on the huffiness, too.

"I'm sure you can understand my reasoning," Franz said now in a crisp voice. "In this business, you can't be too careful."

"I—I suppose not," the official said distractedly. Then he seemed to realize whom he was talking to, and he snapped to attention. "Absolutely not, Monsieur Haussman. You may be sure we will send a truck at the original time."

Now came the tricky part. "My associate and her two secretaries will need to be inside that truck," Franz said firmly. "We're showing them through every step of the Haussman process."

Mr. Balch looked as though he wanted to tear his hair out. "Every step of the— What will riding in an empty truck show them?" he asked.

"You need not concern yourself with that," Franz said icily. "It may seem unusual, but I can assure you it is necessary. Do you have a problem with that?"

"Well, uh—no," said Balch in a defeated voice. "Is there anything else I can do for you?"

He was obviously relieved when Franz told him there wasn't.

"He thinks I'm totally out of my mind, I suppose," Franz said to Nancy when they were safely out of the Schlossinger headquarters. "But he probably thought that before, so it's nothing new. In any case, we have our truck."

Six hours later—at precisely three o'clock in the afternoon—Nancy, Bess, and George were sitting in the back of an armored truck that was about to leave Schlossinger Gold Corporation.

The empty compartment was lit only by a small square of bulletproof glass, and Bess and George were only dark silhouettes next to Nancy. A tense silence surrounded the girls as they waited.

Suddenly Nancy heard the driver shout out something incomprehensible—a goodbye, probably. Then the driver's door slammed and the truck's engine roared to life. With a lurch, Nancy felt the truck pull out of its parking spot.

"D-do you th-think we're going to be all right?" Bess asked nervously.

Nancy tried to put as much comfort into her voice as she could. "I'm sure of it," she said. "What could go wrong?"

"Everything!" Bess answered.

"I hate to say it," George murmured, "but I think she's right."

As Nancy cast her mind back over the previous few hours, she could only cross her fingers and hope that her friends were wrong. In any case, it was too late to change their plan now.

The girls had taken a cab to Schlossingers', found the truck that was scheduled to depart, and climbed in just before it left. The truck was due to arrive at Frères Haussman's service entrance at exactly the time Pascal Haussman's letter to Bart had indicated it would.

Assuming that the timing worked and that Pascal Haussman had in fact tipped off the police that Franz would be trying to steal the gold, the police would be waiting for the truck—and waiting to arrest Franz.

But, of course, there would be no gold inside the truck—nothing at all to steal, in fact. There would only be Nancy and her friends, waiting to expose Pascal and Bart for the crooks they were.

If everything worked out, that was—

"I wish it weren't so dark," Bess whispered again as the truck made a swift turn around a corner. "Do you have any idea where we are, Nan?"

"I've been trying to figure it out by the turns the driver takes," Nancy replied. "It can't be that much longer, though. We're—"

Just then the truck veered violently to the right and jolted to a sudden stop. The three girls were hurled forward onto the floor. Outside the truck, a fierce volley of shouts arose.

"What are they saying? What's happening?" Bess asked nervously, picking herself up off the floor.

"I think Bart and Franz are hijacking the truck now," Nancy said tensely. She had already stood up and was pressing her ear to the side of the truck. "The French is too fast for me to understand it all. Oh, wait—there's another voice. I think it's a police officer questioning them."

The girls didn't have to understand French to recognize the shock in Franz's voice.

"Non! Non! C'est pas moi qui—"

"He's saying he didn't do it," Nancy whispered.

Then Nancy heard the officer's voice announce solemnly, *"Monsieur Haussman, je vous mets aux arrêts."*

"'Mr. Haussman, I'm putting you under arrest,'" Nancy translated rapidly.

Now the girls heard another voice rising above the commotion—Pascal Haussman's voice. He was shouting indignantly at his nephew.

"Quel honte! For shame! You have disgraced us all!"

Abruptly, the voices fell silent. For a fleeting instant, Nancy wondered why. Then all three girls heard the footsteps walking toward the back of the truck.

"Get ready, guys," Nancy whispered to George and Bess.

There was a jingle of keys, then a click as a key slid into the lock at the back of the truck. Nancy heard another click, then a heavy thud as the metal bar holding the door closed was shoved upward.

As the back of the truck swung open, Nancy and her friends blinked at the sudden brightness.

They were staring into the astonished faces of two Swiss police officers, Pascal and Erich Haussman right behind them.

"Qu'est-ce qui arrive?" Pascal Haussman sputtered. "What is going on?"

Before anyone could say another word, Nancy climbed out of the truck. A few feet away, in front of Frères Haussman's service entrance, Franz was struggling in the grip of a third police officer. Nancy didn't see Bart Jackson anywhere.

"You've got the wrong man, officers!" Nancy shouted. She flung her arm out to point at Pascal and his son.

"These are the criminals you're looking for!"

Chapter
Sixteen

"QU'EST-CE QUI ARRIVE?" asked the officer holding Franz, in an incredulous voice. He made no move to relax his hold, Nancy noticed.

She had to give Pascal Haussman credit for steady nerves. His stony expression never wavered. "This is your friend, I believe, Franz?" he asked. "She has a strange sense of humor, I must say." He didn't even glance at George and Bess, who were now climbing quietly out of the back of the truck. The three police officers were staring openmouthed at them.

"You know perfectly well who Nancy is, Uncle," Franz said. "What you *don't* know is that she's a detective. She has been working for me, and she has found out a lot about you and Erich."

Erich flinched nervously, but Pascal didn't

even blink at his nephew's words. He just smiled sadly and turned to the two officers standing behind the truck.

"The poor boy is desperate," Pascal Haussman said. "He'll try anything." One of the officers made a move to speak, but Pascal kept going. "I—I suppose I'm partly responsible for his attitude toward me," he said. "Perhaps I've been too stern with him. I am acting as his guardian while his parents are away, you know."

Pascal's voice throbbed with remorse. "All I can ask, officers, is that you be lenient with him until I find a lawyer." He gave Franz a touching look of concern. "My dear nephew, I won't rest until I've found you the best counsel possible," he said. "There must be an explanation for your sorry behavior. I'm sure that together we can—"

"Good job, Monsieur Haussman," Nancy interrupted sternly. "But not quite good enough."

"Who *is* this young woman?" Pascal asked testily. "Why does she keep interrupting us in this extraordinary way?"

Nancy didn't answer him. Turning to Franz, she asked, "Could you please translate into French for me? I don't want any more misunderstandings."

Franz nodded. As Nancy launched into her explanation, he translated a sentence at a time.

"First of all, officers, let me ask a question. You found Franz stopping the truck—is that right?"

"Yes," one of the police officers replied after Franz had translated for him. "And another man who escaped. *This* one"—he gestured at Franz—"was about to rob the truck."

"Well, you can't arrest Franz for stealing," said Nancy. "There's no gold in the truck, as you can see. Therefore, he's not guilty of theft."

Pascal Haussman began to speak, but Nancy silenced him with a glance. "Think about it, officers. Who could have tipped you off about this heist?" she went on. "Franz certainly wouldn't have—not unless he wanted you to arrest him for some reason. The only people who could have warned you are Pascal or Erich. And the only way they could know a crime was going to take place was if they'd set it up themselves."

Nancy turned back to Pascal. "I had the letters you sent to Bart photocopied yesterday. I figured it wouldn't hurt to have copies. They're very interesting."

The letters weren't conclusive proof of Pascal's guilt, of course. Luckily, Erich Haussman didn't know that.

"Papa!" he cried in a high-pitched, frightened voice. "They know about us! We'll go to jail!"

The look Pascal Haussman gave his son sent chills down Nancy's spine. *"Now* we will, anyway," Pascal said quietly.

Franz stepped forward. This time the officer who'd been restraining him made no move to hold him back.

"Why did you do it, Uncle?" Franz asked. "Why did you want to hurt me so much?"

In that instant Pascal Haussman's steely composure finally cracked. "You can even *ask* that?" he said, pointing a shaking finger at his nephew. "You, who have been such an embarrassment to our family? To our business? What right do you have to inherit half the Haussman fortune?

"Erich is everything you're not," Pascal continued. "Reliable. Hardworking. Steadfast. Why should he have to share anything with you? He deserves it all!"

Franz let out a deep breath. "So that's it," he said. "You didn't want me inheriting my share of the family's fortune."

"No father would want someone like you messing up his own son's future," said Pascal contemptuously. "My poor brother Gunther is deluded to have placed any trust in you."

"He's not the deluded one, Uncle," Franz said sadly. "You are. You really thought it would be all right to frame me—your own nephew—so that Erich would become the sole heir of your company. I wish Papa didn't have to hear about this. It will break his heart."

"You're the one who breaks hearts," his uncle shot back swiftly. "You have been a disappointment to everyone in this family."

Tears of rage were running down Pascal Haussman's face as one of the police officers put a warning hand on his shoulder. Behind him, a trembling Erich was already being slipped into handcuffs.

"You don't deserve Monique!" Erich suddenly

shouted at Franz. "You—you should have given *me* a chance with her."

Franz shook his head sadly. "So that's the reason you hate me—because Monique and I are in love?"

Out of the corner of her eye, Nancy saw a dark blue Mercedes come squealing up to the curb. Mick and an older man jumped out and rushed over to the group.

"Everything went according to plan, I see," Mick said, giving Nancy a quick hug.

Nancy drew a shaky breath. "Yup," she said. "How about you?"

"We've got Bart in the backseat," Mick told her. "Handcuffed, of course. He's not going anywhere now."

"Good work!" Nancy said. Then she turned to Pascal and the police. "You see, sirs, I had a feeling that Bart might try to escape," she said politely. "So I asked my friend Mick to ask *his* friend, the Australian ambassador, to give me a hand."

Nancy nodded at the older man standing next to Mick. He was the same man who'd dropped Mick off at the cathedral a couple of days before. "Mick and the ambassador followed the armored truck until it was stopped," Nancy continued. "Bart tried to escape, of course, but Mick managed to catch him."

"I chased him down an alley," Mick said. "Luckily for me it turned out to be a dead end."

"A dead end," Nancy repeated. She stared first at Pascal Haussman, who was gritting his teeth then at Erich, who was wiping his eyes with the back of his hand, and finally at Bart Jackson, who was glaring at them from the back of the ambassador's car.

"It was a dead end in more ways than one, I'd say."

"Well, I can see why your family's chocolates are so famous, Monique," Nancy said on Saturday evening. She took a shell-shaped truffle from the box Monique was handing around and bit into it. "Mmm. These are the best I've ever had!"

To celebrate the end of the case, Franz, Monique, Nancy, Bess, George, and Mick had decided to go out to dinner at one of Geneva's best restaurants. After a meal that combined the best of French cuisine with the best of German, they were all sitting around the table nibbling on the chocolates Monique had brought with her.

"Forget about chocolate for a while. I'd like to make a toast," Franz said. He raised a brimming glass and smiled at everyone around the table. "To Nancy, Bess, and George, for their superb help in restoring my reputation—which certainly needed it," he joked.

Turning to Mick, he added, "To Mick Devlin, a good friend who's not afraid to use his connections."

Then Franz stared deeply into Monique's eyes. "And to Monique—the most wonderful girlfriend any man could have. And now, I am happy to announce, the most wonderful wife this man *will* have."

"You're engaged!" Bess squealed as everyone at the table burst into applause. "Oh, that's fantastic!"

"It certainly is," Nancy echoed. "When did this happen, Franz?"

Franz beamed at Nancy. "This afternoon," he said. "I realized that my uncle was right—about one thing, anyway. I have been wasting Monique's time. It's time for me to stop playing jet-setter and settle down." He smiled tenderly at Monique. "Not that that will be hard to learn, with Monique to help me," he said.

It would have been a perfect evening, Nancy thought, except for the lingering sadness in the fact that they were here only because Franz's uncle and cousin—as well as Bart Jackson— were now behind bars. Franz had visited his relatives in jail that afternoon, and the story he'd related to Nancy afterward hadn't been a happy one.

"How did your uncle seem this afternoon when you visited him?" Mick asked Franz as if he were reading Nancy's mind.

"Pathetic," Franz said sadly. "And as for Erich"—he shook his head—"I'm not sure he'll ever recover. He's had some kind of break-down."

"Well, I hope you don't feel sorry for Bart," Bess said tartly. "After all, he did try to push Nancy out of that train window. *And* almost drown her with that cruiser of Monique's father. He says he wasn't trying to kill anyone, only scare Franz into cooperating with him. I don't buy that though."

"I do," said Nancy. "Just think, why would he kill the person he was hired to set up. He'd never get paid. He also could have pushed me all the way out the train window, but he didn't. I believe he was just trying to scare us."

Mick shuddered and gave Nancy a quick squeeze when she mentioned the train again. "Erich told Bart we were on the train, I assume?" he asked.

"That's right," Nancy said, remembering what Franz had told her following his visit to the police station. "By the way, the reason Erich was so upset when Franz disappeared wasn't that he was worried for Franz's safety. He was just worried because Franz had skipped town without Bart knowing it."

"So he was worried because he thought Franz *would* be safe," said Mick dryly. "I can't believe we actually helped him find you, Franz. Don't tell me he was the one who pushed that boulder down the Matterhorn?"

"No," Nancy answered for Franz. "That was Bart. And it was Bart who pushed Franz into the lake at the party. He's confessed to everything."

Bess shook her head in amazement. "Why didn't any of us notice him there?" asked Bess. "You'd think *one* of us would have."

"Erich had him put on a waiter's jacket," Franz told her. "People almost never notice the staff at a big party like that."

Bess shivered and glanced behind her at the waiter who was hovering over their table. "Well, I'm going to *start* noticing," she said.

Monique smiled. "Perhaps you will become a detective, too, then."

"No way," Bess said firmly. "Things get hairy enough just helping Nancy out from time to time!"

"Let's hope Nancy can get a break from detecting in Rome, at least," George put in, grinning at her across the table. "I think you need a vacation from your vacation, Nan."

"Oh, are you going to Rome next?" Monique inquired.

Nancy nodded, suddenly feeling inexplicably sad. "I wish we could stay in Geneva longer, but it's time for us to move on. We've only got one summer in Europe."

"I hate to see you go so soon," Monique said wistfully. "But as long as it's Rome you're going to, you should look up my friend Claudia Beluggi. Remember meeting her? She lives in Rome, and I'm sure she'd love to show you around."

The three girls smiled. "As a matter of fact, we already got in touch with Claudia," said Nancy. "I called her this afternoon, just to see if she remembered inviting us. Luckily, she did. We're going to get together as soon as we arrive."

"Oh, you will have a wonderful time," Monique said. "Rome is a fantastic city." She turned to Franz. "Perhaps we should go along."

But Franz shook his head. "We need to plan our wedding," he said. "I want to surprise my parents when they come home." Wrapping an arm around his fiancée, he drew her closer to him. "We'll have a whole lifetime to travel together, Monique," he said. "And I'm sure that we'll meet our new friends again."

"You were awfully quiet at dinner, Mick," Nancy commented about an hour later.

Mick sighed. "I didn't have much to say. I'm going to Paris on the night train, you're off to Rome. Who knows when or if we'll see each other again?"

Dinner was over. Franz and Monique had gone home, and Bess and George had taken a cab back to the hotel so they could finish packing. They had discreetly left Nancy and Mick to catch their own cab—but Nancy and Mick had decided to walk back instead. It was a way to prolong the time they had left together, and a way to finish saying the things they needed to say to each other.

"I don't suppose you'd consider changing your plans?" Mick asked. "Paris is a beautiful city. It would be fun to see it together."

Nancy gave him a rueful smile. "I can't do it, Mick. And not only because my friends and I have already made our plans to see Rome." Taking Mick's hand in hers, she gave it a squeeze. "You're a wonderful person," she said softly. "There's something very special between us."

A look of longing sprang into Mick's eyes.

"You feel it, too?" he asked. "Then why can't we—"

Nancy reached up and put her finger to his lips. "It wouldn't work," she said. "I've got—commitments back home."

She was thinking of Ned. She wasn't sure how she felt about her boyfriend right then, but she knew she couldn't just forget all about him. She vowed to write him a long letter the first chance she got.

"Besides," Nancy added gently, "we're headed in different directions."

"I guess you're right," Mick said. "But that doesn't mean we can't say goodbye properly."

He leaned forward, and they exchanged a lingering kiss.

"I'll miss you," Mick said in a husky voice.

"And I'll miss you," Nancy whispered back.

It was the truth. Still, sad as she was to bid Mick goodbye, Nancy couldn't help being happy at the thought of the adventures that lay ahead of her that summer. She was off to Rome—and then, who could say?

Europe lay ahead of Nancy and her friends like a shimmering treasure map. Nancy couldn't wait to see what was in store for them next.

Next in the Passport to Romance Trilogy:

As their European summer continues, Nancy, Bess, and George find that all roads lead to Rome—the city of artistic wonders, great-looking guys, and chic boutiques. But when an innocent shopping spree makes them the target of a cunning crime spree, they realize that one wrong turn could lead them straight down the road to ruin!

Bess lays down a few *lire* for an imitation Etruscan necklace and finds she's bought much more than she bargained for. The jewelry turns out to be the real thing: real old, real valuable, and real hot. Nancy vows to find out who planted the necklace and who is trying to steal it back. But the truth is as dangerous as it is elusive . . . and now it's Nancy's neck that is on the line . . . in *RENDEZVOUS IN ROME*, Case #73 in the Nancy Drew Files™.